A Wind in the Door

By Madeleine L'Engle

A Wind in the Door

❋

MADELEINE L'ENGLE

Quality Paperback Book Club
New York

The author wishes to acknowledge that it was the kind interest of the
Children's Book Council, Inc., in 1970, that aroused the germinal impulse
which has resulted in the writing of this book.

Printed in the United States of America

For Pat

THE L'ENGLE

THOSE WHO CROSS AND CONNECT
CHRONOS ** AND *KAIROS* *

Canon Tallis
The Arm of the Starfish, The Young Unicorns,
A Circle of Quiet, The Summer of the Great-grandmother,
Dragons in the Waters, The Irrational Season, Walking on Water

Adam Eddington
(Starfish, Light)

Mr. Theotocopoulous
(Unicorns, Dragons)

Katherine Forrester = Justin Michel Vigneras
(A Severed Wasp, The Small Rain)

Felix Bodeway
(Wasp, Rain)

Zachary Gray
(Lotus, Moon, Light, Acceptable)

Virginia Bowen Porcher
(A Winter's Love, Lotus)

Frank Rowan
(Camilla, Lotus)

Emily Gregory
(Wasp, Unicorns)

Philippa Hunter
(Wasp, And Both Were Young)

Theron Renier = Stella
(The Other Side of the Sun)

Leonis Phair
(Dragons)

Simon Renier
(Dragons)

Mimi Renier
Oppenheimer
(Wasp)

Queron Renier
"Renny"
(Lotus)

*Kairos is real time, pure numbers with no measurement.
**Chronos is ordinary, wrist-watch, alarm-clock time.

FAMILY TREE

THE MURRY-O'KEEFES, *KAIROS* *

A Wrinkle in Time, A Wind in the Door, A Swiftly Tilting Planet, Many Waters, An Acceptable Time

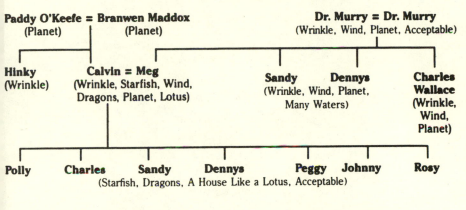

Paddy O'Keefe = Branwen Maddox
(Planet)   (Planet)

Dr. Murry = Dr. Murry
(Wrinkle, Wind, Planet, Acceptable)

Hinky
(Wrinkle)

Calvin = Meg
(Wrinkle, Starfish, Wind,
Dragons, Planet, Lotus)

Sandy   Dennys
(Wrinkle, Wind, Planet,
Many Waters)

Charles
Wallace
(Wrinkle,
Wind,
Planet)

Polly   Charles   Sandy   Dennys   Peggy   Johnny   Rosy
(Starfish, Dragons, A House Like a Lotus, Acceptable)

THE AUSTINS, *CHRONOS* * *

Meet the Austins, The Moon by Night, The Twenty-four Days before Christmas,
The Young Unicorns, A Ring of Endless Light, The Anti-Muffins

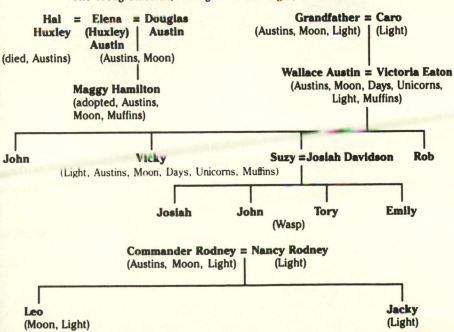

Hal = Elena = Douglas
Huxley (Huxley) Austin
         Austin

(died, Austins)   (Austins, Moon)

Grandfather = Caro
(Austins, Moon, Light) (Light)

Maggy Hamilton
(adopted, Austins,
Moon, Muffins)

Wallace Austin = Victoria Eaton
(Austins, Moon, Days, Unicorns,
Light, Muffins)

John   Vicky   Suzy = Josiah Davidson   Rob
        (Light, Austins, Moon, Days, Unicorns, Muffins)

Josiah   John   Tory   Emily
          (Wasp)

Commander Rodney = Nancy Rodney
(Austins, Moon, Light)   (Light)

Leo   Jacky
(Moon, Light)   (Light)

Contents

A Wind in the Door

"What, nephew," said the king,
"is the wind in that door?"
SIR THOMAS MALORY
Le Morte d'Arthur

1 Charles Wallace's Dragons

"There are dragons in the twins' vegetable garden."

Meg Murry took her head out of the refrigerator where she had been foraging for an after-school snack, and looked at her six-year-old brother. "What?"

"There are dragons in the twins' vegetable garden. Or there were. They've moved to the north pasture now."

Meg, not replying—it did not do to answer Charles Wallace too quickly when he said something odd—returned to the refrigerator. "I suppose I'll have lettuce and tomato as usual. I was looking for something new and different and exciting."

"Meg, did you hear me?"

"Yes, I heard you. I think I'll have liverwurst and cream cheese." She took her sandwich materials and a bottle of milk and set them out on the kitchen table. Charles Wallace waited patiently. She looked at him, scowling with an anxiety she did not like to admit to herself, at the fresh rips in the knees of his blue jeans, the streaks of dirt grained deep in his shirt, a darkening bruise on the cheekbone under his left eye. "Okay, did the big boys jump you in the schoolyard this time, or when you got off the bus?"

3

"Meg, you aren't listening to me."

"I happen to care that you've been in school for two months now and not a single week has gone by that you haven't been roughed up. If you've been talking about dragons in the garden or wherever they are, I suppose that explains it."

"I haven't. Don't underestimate me. I didn't see them till I got home."

Whenever Meg was deeply worried she got angry. Now she scowled at her sandwich. "I wish Mother'd get the spreadable kind of cream cheese. This stuff keeps going right through the bread. Where is she?"

"In the lab, doing an experiment. She said to tell you she wouldn't be long."

"Where's Father?"

"He got a call from L.A., and he's gone to Washington for a couple of days."

Like the dragons in the garden, their father's visits to the White House were something best not talked about at school. Unlike the dragons, these visits were real.

Charles Wallace picked up Meg's doubting. "But I saw them, Meg, the dragons. Eat your sandwich and come see."

"Where're Sandy and Dennys?"

"Soccer practice. I haven't told anybody but you." Suddenly sounding forlorn, younger than his six years, he said, "I wish the high-school bus got home earlier. I've been waiting and waiting for you."

Meg returned to the refrigerator to get lettuce. This was a cover for some rapid thinking, although she couldn't

4

count on Charles Wallace not picking up her thoughts, as he had picked up her doubts about the dragons. What he had actually seen she could not begin to guess. That he had seen something, something unusual, she was positive.

Charles Wallace silently watched her finish making the sandwich, carefully aligning the slices of bread and cutting it in precise sections. "I wonder if Mr. Jenkins has ever seen a dragon?"

Mr. Jenkins was the principal of the village school, and Meg had had her own troubles with him. She had small hope that Mr. Jenkins would care what happened to Charles Wallace, or that he would be willing to interfere in what he called 'the normal procedures of democracy.' "Mr. Jenkins believes in the law of the jungle." She spoke through a mouthful. "Aren't there dragons in the jungle?"

Charles Wallace finished his glass of milk. "No wonder you always flunk social studies. Eat your sandwich and stop stalling. Let's go and see if they're still there."

They crossed the lawn, followed by Fortinbras, the large, black, almost-Labrador dog, happily sniffing and snuffling at the rusty autumnal remains of the rhubarb patch. Meg tripped over a wire hoop from the croquet set, and made an annoyed grunt, mostly at herself, because she had put the wickets and mallets away after the last game, and forgotten this one. A low wall of barberry separated the croquet lawn from Sandy's and Dennys's vegetable garden. Fortinbras leaped over the barberry, and Meg called automatically, "Not in the garden, Fort," and the big dog backed out, between rows of cabbage and broccoli. The twins were justly proud of their organic produce, which they sold around the village for pocket money.

"A dragon could make a real mess of this garden," Charles Wallace said, and led Meg through rows of vegetables. "I think he realized that, because suddenly he sort of wasn't there."

"What do you mean, he sort of wasn't there? Either he was there, or he wasn't."

"He was there, and then when I went to look closer, he wasn't there, and I followed him—not really him, because he was much faster than I, and I only followed where he'd been. And he went to the big glacial rocks in the north pasture."

Meg looked scowlingly at the garden. Never before had Charles Wallace sounded as implausible as this.

He said, "Come on," and moved past the tall sheaves of corn, which had only a few scraggly ears left. Beyond the corn the sunflowers caught the slanting rays of the afternoon sun, their golden faces reflecting brilliance.

"Charles, are you all right?" Meg asked. It was not like Charles to lose touch with reality. Then she noticed that he was breathing heavily, as if he had been running, though they had not been walking rapidly. His face was pale, his forehead beaded with perspiration, as though from over-exertion.

She did not like the way he looked, and she turned her mind back to the unlikely tale of dragons, picking her way around the luxuriant pumpkin vines. "Charles, when did you see these—dragons?"

"A dollop of dragons, a drove of dragons, a drive of dragons," Charles Wallace panted. "After I got home from school. Mother was all upset because I looked such a mess. My nose was still very bloody."

"I get upset, too."

"Meg, Mother thinks it's more than the bigger kids punching me."

"What's more?"

Charles Wallace scrambled with unusual clumsiness and difficulty over the low stone wall which edged the orchard. "I get out of breath."

Meg said sharply, "Why? What did Mother say?"

Charles walked slowly through the high grass in the orchard. "She hasn't *said*. But it's sort of like radar blipping at me."

Meg walked beside him. She was tall for her age, and Charles Wallace small for his. "There are times when I wish you didn't pick up radar signals quite so well."

"I can't help it, Meg. I don't try to. It just happens. Mother thinks something is wrong with me."

"But what?" she almost shouted.

Charles Wallace spoke very quietly. "I don't know. Something bad enough so her worry blips loud and clear. And I know there's something wrong. Just to walk across the orchard like this is an effort, and it shouldn't be. It never has been before."

"When did this start?" she asked sharply. "You were all right last weekend when we went walking in the woods."

"I know. I've been sort of tired all autumn, but it's been worse this week, and much worse today than it was yes-

7

terday. Hey, Meg! Stop blaming yourself because you didn't notice."

She had been doing precisely that. Her hands felt cold with panic. She tried to push her fear away, because Charles Wallace could read his sister even more easily than he could their mother. He picked up a windfall apple, looked it over for worms, and bit into it. His end-of-summer tan could not disguise his extreme pallor, nor his shadowed eyes; why hadn't she noticed this? Because she hadn't wanted to. It was easier to blame Charles Wallace's paleness and lethargy on his problems at school.

"Why doesn't Mother have a doctor look at you, then? I mean a real doctor?"

"She has."

"When?"

"Today."

"Why didn't you tell me before?"

"I was more interested in dragons."

"Charles!"

"It was before you got home from school. Dr. Louise came to have lunch with Mother—she does, quite often, anyhow—"

"I know. Go on."

"So when I got home from school she went over me, from top to toe."

"What did she say?"

"Nothing much. I can't read her the way I can read Mother. She's like a little bird, twittering away, and all the time you know that sharp mind of hers is thinking along on another level. She's very good at blocking me. All I could gather was that she thought Mother might be right about—about whatever it is. And she'd keep in touch."

They had finished crossing the orchard and Charles Wallace climbed up onto the wall again and stood there, looking across an unused pasture where there were two large outcroppings of glacial rock. "They're gone," he said. "My dragons are gone."

Meg stood on the wall beside him. There was nothing to see except the wind blowing through the sun-bleached grasses, and the two tall rocks, turning purple in the autumn evening light. "Are you sure it wasn't just the rocks or shadows or something?"

"Do rocks or shadows look like dragons?"

"No, but—"

"Meg, they were right by the rocks, all sort of clustered together, wings, it looked like hundreds of wings, and eyes opening and shutting between the wings, and some smoke and little spurts of fire, and I warned them not to set the pasture on fire."

"How did you warn them?"

"I spoke to them. In a loud voice. And the flames stopped."

"Did you go close?"

"It didn't seem wise. I stayed here on the wall and watched for a long time. They kept folding and unfolding wings and sort of winking all those eyes at me, and then they all seemed to huddle together and go to sleep, so I went home to wait for you. Meg! You don't believe me."

9

She asked, flatly, "Well, where have they gone?"

"You've never not believed me before."

She said, carefully, "It's not that I don't believe you." In a strange way she did believe him. Not, perhaps, that he had seen actual dragons—but Charles Wallace had never before tended to mix fact and fancy. Never before had he separated reality and illusion in such a marked way. She looked at him, saw that he had a sweatshirt on over his grubby shirt. She held her arms about herself, shivered, and said—although she was quite warm enough—"I think I'll go back to the house and get a cardigan. Wait here. I won't be long. If the dragons come back—"

"I think they will come back."

"Then keep them here for me. I'll be as fast as I can."

Charles Wallace looked at her levelly. "I don't think Mother wants to be interrupted right now."

"I'm not going to interrupt her. I'm just going to get my cardigan."

"Okay, Meg," he sighed.

She left him sitting on the wall, looking at the two great glacial deposits, waiting for dragons, or whatever it was he thought he'd seen. All right, he knew that she was going back to the house to talk to their mother, but as long as she didn't admit it out loud she felt that she managed to keep at least a little of her worry from him.

She burst into the laboratory.

Her mother was sitting on a tall lab stool, not looking into the microscope in front of her, not writing on the clip-

10

board which rested on her knee, just sitting thoughtfully. "What is it, Meg?"

She started to blurt out Charles Wallace's talk of dragons, and that he had never had delusions before, but since Charles Wallace himself had not mentioned them to their mother, it seemed like a betrayal for her to do so, though his silence about the dragons may have been because of the presence of Dr. Louise.

Her mother repeated, a little impatiently, "What is it, Meg?"

"What's wrong with Charles Wallace?"

Mrs. Murry put the clipboard down on the lab counter beside the microscope. "He had some trouble with the bigger boys again in school today."

"That's not what I mean."

"What do you mean, Meg?"

"He said you had Dr. Colubra here for him."

"Louise was here for lunch, so I thought she might as well have a look at him."

"And?"

"And what, Meg?"

"What's the matter with him?"

"We don't know, Meg. Not yet, at any rate."

"Charles says you're worried about him."

"I am. Aren't you?"

"Yes. But I thought it was all school. And now I don't think it is. He got out of breath just walking across the orchard. And he's too pale. And he imagines things. And he looks—I don't like the way he looks."

11

"Neither do I."

"What is it? What's wrong? Is it a virus or something?"

Mrs. Murry hesitated. "I'm not sure."

"Mother, please, if there's anything really wrong with Charles I'm old enough to know."

"I don't know whether there is or not. Neither does Louise. When we find out anything definite, I'll tell you. I promise you that."

"You're not hiding anything?"

"Meg, there's no use talking about something I'm not sure of. I should know in a few days."

Meg twisted her hands together nervously. "You really are worried."

Mrs. Murry smiled. "Mothers tend to be. Where is he now?"

"Oh—I left him on the stone wall—I said I was coming in for a cardigan. I've got to run back or he'll think—" Without finishing she rushed out of the lab, grabbed a cardigan from one of the hooks in the pantry, and ran across the lawn.

When she reached Charles Wallace he was sitting on the wall, just as she had left him. There was no sign of dragons.

She had not really expected that there would be. Nevertheless, she was disappointed, her anxiety about Charles subtly deepened.

"What did Mother say?" he asked.

"Nothing."

His large, deep-seeing blue eyes focused on her. "She didn't mention mitochondria? Or farandolae?"

"Hunh? Why should she?"

Charles Wallace kicked the rubber heels of his sneakers against the wall, looked at Meg, did not answer.

Meg persisted, "Why should Mother mention mitochondria? Isn't that—talking about them—what got you into trouble your very first day in school?"

"I am extremely interested in them. And in dragons. I'm sorry they haven't come back yet." He was very definitely changing the subject. "Let's wait a while longer for them. I'd rather face a few dragons any day than the kids in the schoolyard. Thank you for going to see Mr. Jenkins on my behalf, Meg."

That was supposed to be a deep, dark secret. "How did you know?"

"I knew."

Meg hunched her shoulders. "Not that it did any good." She had not really had much hope that it would. Mr. Jenkins had been, for several years, the principal of the large regional high school. When he was moved, just that September, to the small grade school in the village, the official story was that the school needed upgrading, and Mr. Jenkins was the only man to do the job. The rumor was that he hadn't been able to handle the wilder element over at Regional. Meg had her doubts whether or not he could handle anybody, anywhere. And she was completely convinced that he would neither understand nor like Charles Wallace.

The morning that Charles Wallace set off for first grade, Meg was far more nervous than he was. She could not concentrate during her last classes, and when school was finally over and she climbed the hill to the house and found him with a puffed and bleeding upper lip and a scrape across his cheek, she had a sinking feeling of inevitability combined with a burning rage. Charles Wallace had always been thought of by the villagers as peculiar, and probably not quite all there. Meg, picking up mail at the post office, or eggs at the store, overheard snatches of conversations: 'That littlest Murry kid is a weird one.' 'I hear clever people often have dumb kids.' 'They say he can't even talk.'

It would have been easier if Charles Wallace had actually been stupid. But he wasn't, and he wasn't very good at pretending that he didn't know more than the other six-year-olds in his class. His vocabulary itself was against him; he had, in fact, not started talking until late, but then it was in complete sentences, with none of the baby preliminaries. In front of strangers he still seldom spoke at all—one of the reasons he was thought dumb; and suddenly there he was in first grade and talking like—like his parents, or his sister. Sandy and Dennys got along with everybody. It wasn't surprising that Charles was resented; everybody expected him to be backward, and he talked like a dictionary.

"Now, children"—the first-grade teacher smiled brightly at the gaggle of new first-graders staring at her that first morning—"I want each one of you to tell me something about yourselves." She looked at her list. "Let's start with Mary Agnes. Which one is Mary Agnes?"

A small girl with one missing front tooth, and straw-colored hair pulled tightly into pigtails, announced that she lived on a farm and that she had her own chickens; that morning there had been seventeen eggs.

"Very *good,* Mary Agnes. Now, let's see, how about you, Richard—are you called Dicky?"

A fat little boy stood up, bobbing and grinning.

"What have *you* got to tell us?"

"Boys ain't like girls," Dicky said. "Boys is made different, see, like—"

"That's *fine,* Dicky, just fine. We'll learn more about that later. Now, Albertina, suppose you tell us something."

Albertina was repeating first grade. She stood up, almost a head taller than the others, and announced proudly, "Our bodies are made up of bones and skinses and muskle and blood cells and stuff like that."

"Very *good,* Albertina. Isn't that good, class? I can see we're going to have a group of real scientists this year. Let's all clap for Albertina, shall we? Now, uh"—she looked down at her list again—"Charles Wallace. Are you called Charlie?"

"No," he said. "Charles Wallace, please."

"Your parents are scientists, aren't they?" She did not wait for an answer. "Let's see what *you* have to tell us."

Charles Wallace ('You should have known better!' Meg scolded him that night) stood and said, "What I'm interested in right now are the farandolae and the mitochondria."

"What was that, Charles? The mighty what?"

"Mitochondria. They and the farandolae come from the prokaryocytes—"

15

"The *what?*"

"Well, billions of years ago they probably swam into what eventually became our eukaryotic cells and they've just stayed there. They have their own DNA and RNA, which means they're quite separate from us. They have a symbiotic relationship with us, and the amazing thing is that we're completely dependent on them for our oxygen."

"Now, Charles, suppose you stop making silly things up, and the next time I call on you, don't try to show off. Now, George, you tell the class something . . ."

At the end of the second week of school, Charles Wallace paid Meg an evening visit in her attic bedroom.

"Charles," she said, "can't you just not say anything at all?"

Charles Wallace, in yellow footed pajamas, his fresh wounds band-aided, his small nose looking puffy and red, lay on the foot of Meg's big brass bed, his head pillowed on the shiny black bulk of the dog, Fortinbras. He sounded weary, and lethargic, although she hadn't noticed this at the time. "It doesn't work. Nothing works. If I don't talk, I'm sulking. If I talk I say something wrong. I've finished the workbook—the teacher said you must've helped me— and I know the reader by heart."

Meg, circling her knees with her arms, looked down at boy and dog; Fortinbras was strictly not allowed on beds, but this rule was ignored in the attic. "Why don't they move you up to second grade?"

"That would be even worse. They're that much bigger than I "

Yes. She knew that was true.

So she decided to go see Mr. Jenkins. She boarded the high-school bus as usual at seven o'clock, in the grey, uninviting light of an early morning brewing a nor'easter. The grade-school bus, which had not nearly so far to go, left an hour later. When the high-school bus made its first stop in the village she slipped off, and then walked the two miles to the grade school. It was an old, inadequate building, painted the traditional red, overcrowded and understaffed. It certainly did need upgrading, and taxes were being raised for a new school.

She slipped through the side door which the custodian opened early. She could hear the buzz of his electric floor polisher in the front hall by the still-locked entrance doors, and under cover of its busy sound she ran across the hall and darted into a small broom closet and leaned, too noisily for comfort, against the hanging brooms and dry mops. The closet smelled musty and dusty and she hoped she could keep from sneezing until Mr. Jenkins was in his office and his secretary had brought him his ritual mug of coffee. She shifted position and leaned against the corner, where she could see the glass top of the door to Mr. Jenkins's office through the narrow crack.

She was stuffy-nosed and cramp-legged when the light in the office finally went on. Then she waited for what seemed all day but was more like half an hour, while she

listened to the click of the secretary's heels on the polished
tile floor, then the roar of children entering the school as
the doors were unlocked. She thought of Charles Wallace
being pushed along by the great wave of children, mostly
much bigger than he was.

—It's like the mob after Julius Caesar, she thought,—
only Charles isn't much like Caesar. But I'll bet life was
simpler when all Gaul was divided in three parts.

The bell screamed for the beginning of classes. The secretary clicked along the corridor again. That would be with
Mr. Jenkins's coffee. The high heels receded. Meg waited
for what she calculated was five minutes, then emerged,
pressing her forefinger against her upper lip to stifle a
sneeze. She crossed the corridor and knocked on Mr.
Jenkins's door, just as the sneeze burst out anyhow.

He seemed surprised to see her, as well he might, and
not at all pleased, though his actual words were, "May I
ask to what I owe this pleasure?"

"I need to see you, please, Mr. Jenkins."

"Why aren't you in school?"

"I am. This school."

"Kindly don't be rude, Meg. I see you haven't changed
any over the summer. I had hoped you would not be one of
my problems this year. Have you informed anybody of
your whereabouts?" The early morning light glinted off his
spectacles, veiling his eyes. Meg pushed her own spectacles
up her nose, but could not read his expression; as usual,
she thought, he looked as though he smelled something unpleasant.

18

He sniffed. "I will have my secretary drive you to school. That will mean the loss of her services for a full half day."

"I'll hitchhike, thanks."

"Compounding one misdemeanor with another? In this state, hitchhiking happens to be against the law."

"Mr. Jenkins, I didn't come to talk to you about hitch-hiking, I came to talk to you about Charles Wallace."

"I don't appreciate your interference, Margaret."

"The bigger boys are bullying him. They'll really hurt him if you don't stop them."

"If anybody is dissatisfied with my handling of the situation and wishes to discuss it with me, I think it should be your parents."

Meg tried to control herself, but her voice rose with frustrated anger. "Maybe they're cleverer than I am and know it won't do any good. Oh, please, please, Mr. Jenkins, I know people have thought Charles Wallace isn't very bright, but he's really—"

He cut across her words. "We've run IQ tests on all the first-graders. Your little brother's IQ is quite satisfactory."

"You know it's more than that, Mr. Jenkins. My parents have run tests on him, too, all kinds of tests. His IQ is so high it's untestable by normal standards."

"His performance gives no indication of this."

"Don't you understand, he's trying to hold back so the boys won't beat him up? He doesn't understand them, and they don't understand him. How many first-graders know about farandolae?"

"I don't know what you're talking about, Margaret. I do

19

know that Charles Wallace does not seem to me to be very strong."

"He's perfectly all right!"

"He is extremely pale, and there are dark circles under his eyes."

"How would *you* look if people punched you in the nose and kept giving you black eyes just because you know more than they do?"

"If he's so bright"—Mr. Jenkins looked coldly at her through the magnifying lenses of his spectacles—"I wonder your parents bother to send him to school at all?"

"If there weren't a law about it, they probably wouldn't."

Now, standing by Charles Wallace on the stone wall, looking at the two glacial rocks where no dragons lurked, Meg recalled Mr. Jenkins's words about Charles Wallace's pallor, and shivered.

Charles asked, "Why do people always mistrust people who are different? Am I really that different?"

Meg, moving the tip of her tongue over her teeth which had only recently lost their braces, looked at him affectionately and sadly. "Oh, Charles, I don't know. I'm your sister. I've known you ever since you were born. I'm too close to you to know." She sat on the stone wall, first carefully checking the rocks: a large, gentle, and completely harmless black snake lived in the stone wall. She was a special pet of the twins, and they had watched her grow from a small snakelet to her present flourishing size. She was named Louise, after Dr. Louise Colubra, because the twins had learned just enough Latin to pounce on the odd last name.

"Dr. Snake," Dennys had said. "Weirdo."

"It's a nice name," Sandy said. "We'll name our snake after her. Louise the Larger."

"Why the Larger?"

"Why not?"

"Does she have to be larger than anything?"

"She is."

"She certainly isn't larger than Dr. Louise."

Dennys bristled. "Louise the Larger is very large for a snake who lives in a garden wall, and Dr. Louise is a very small doctor—I mean, she's a tiny person. I suppose as a doctor she's pretty mammoth."

"Well, doctors don't have to be any size. But you're right, Den, she is tiny. And our snake is big." The twins seldom disagreed about anything for long.

"The only trouble is, she's more like a bird than a snake."

"Didn't snakes and birds, way back in evolution, didn't they evolve originally from the same phylum, or whatever you call it? Anyhow, Louise is a very good name for our snake."

Dr. Louise, fortunately, was highly amused. Snakes were misunderstood creatures, she told the twins, and she was honored to have such a handsome one named after her. And snakes, she added, were on the caduceus, which is the emblem for doctors, so it was all most appropriate.

Louise the Larger had grown considerably since her baptism, and Meg, though not actively afraid of her, was always careful to look for Louise before she sat. Louise, at this moment, was nowhere to be seen, so Meg relaxed and turned her thoughts again to Charles Wallace. "You're a lot brighter than the twins, but the twins are far from dumb. How do *they* manage?"

Charles Wallace said, "I wish they'd tell me."

"They don't talk at school the way they do at home, for one thing."

"I thought if I was interested in mitochondria and farandolae, other people would be, too."

"You were wrong."

"I really *am* interested in them. Why is that so peculiar?"

"I don't suppose it *is* so peculiar for the son of a physicist and a biologist."

"Most people aren't. Interested, I mean."

"They aren't children of two scientists, either. Our parents provide us with all kinds of disadvantages. I'll never be as beautiful as Mother."

Charles Wallace was tired of reassuring Meg. "And the incredible thing about farandolae is their size."

Meg was thinking about her hair, the ordinary straight brown of a field mouse, as against her mother's auburn waves. "What about it?"

"They're so small that all anyone can do is postulate them; even the most powerful micro-electron microscope can't show them. But they're important to us—we'd die if we didn't have farandolae. But nobody at school is remotely interested. Our teacher has the mind of a grasshopper. As you were saying, it's not an advantage having famous parents."

"If they weren't famous—you bet everybody knows when L.A. calls, or Father makes a trip to the White House—they'd be in for it too. We're all different, our family. Except the twins. They do all right. Maybe because they're normal. Or know how to act it. But then I wonder what normal is, anyhow, or isn't? Why are you so interested in farandolae?"

"Mother's working on them."

"She's worked on lots of things and you haven't been this interested."

"If she really proves their existence, she'll probably get the Nobel Prize."

"So? That's not what's bugging you about them."

"Meg, if something happens to our farandolae—well, it would be disastrous."

"Why?" Meg shivered, suddenly cold, and buttoned her cardigan. Clouds were scudding across the sky, and with them a rising wind.

"I mentioned mitochondria, didn't I?"

"You did. What about them?"

"Mitochondria are tiny little organisms living in our cells. That gives you an idea of how tiny they are, doesn't it?"

"Enough."

"A human being is a whole world to a mitochondrion, just the way our planet is to us. But we're much more dependent on our mitochondria than the earth is on us. The

23

earth could get along perfectly well without people, but if anything happened to our mitochondria, we'd die."

"Why should anything happen to them?"

Charles Wallace gave a small shrug. In the darkening light he looked very pale. "Accidents happen to people. Or diseases. Things can happen to anything. But what I've sort of picked up from Mother is that quite a lot of mito-chondria are in some kind of trouble because of their faran-dolae."

"Has Mother actually told you all this?"

"Some of it. The rest I've just—gathered."

Charles Wallace did gather things out of his mother's mind, out of Meg's mind, as another child might gather daisies in a field. "What are farandolae, then?" She shifted position on the hard rocks of the wall.

"Farandolae live in a mitochondrion sort of the same way a mitochondrion lives in a human cell. They're genetically independent of their mitochondria, just as mitochondria are of us. And if anything happens to the farandolae in a mitochondrion, the mitochondrion gets—gets sick. And probably dies."

A dry leaf separated from its stem and drifted past Meg's cheek. "Why should anything happen to them?" she repeated.

Charles Wallace repeated, too, "Accidents happen to people, don't they? And disease. And people killing each other in wars."

"Yes, but that's people. Why are you going on so about mitochondria and farandolae?"

24

"Meg, Mother's been working in her lab, night and day, almost literally, for several weeks now. You've noticed that."

"She often does when she's on to something."

"She's on to farandolae. She thinks she's proved their existence by studying some mitochondria, mitochondria which are dying."

"You're not talking about all this stuff at school, are you?"

"I do learn some things, Meg. You aren't really listening to me."

"I'm worried about you."

"Then *listen*. The reason Mother's been in her lab so much trying to find the effect of farandolae on mitochondria is that she thinks there's something wrong with my mitochondria."

"What?" Meg jumped down from the stone wall and swung around to face her brother.

He spoke very quietly, so that she had to bend down to hear. "If my mitochondria get sick, then so do I."

All the fear which Meg had been trying to hold back threatened to break loose. "How serious is it? Can Mother give you something for it?"

"I don't know. She won't talk to me. I'm only guessing. She's trying to shut me out till she knows more, and I can only get in through the chinks. Maybe it's not really serious. Maybe it's all just school; I really do get punched or knocked down almost every day. It's enough to make me feel— Hey—look at Louise!"

Meg turned, following his gaze. Louise the Larger was slithering along the stones of the wall towards them, moving rapidly, sinuously, her black curves shimmering purple and silver in the autumn light. Meg cried, "Charles! Quick!"

He did not move. "She won't hurt us."

"Charles, run! She's going to attack!"

But Louise stopped her advance, just a few feet from Charles Wallace, and raised herself up, uncoiling until she stood, barely on the last few inches of her length, rearing up and looking around expectantly.

Charles Wallace said, "There's someone near. Someone Louise knows."

"The—the dragons?"

"I don't know. I can't see anything. Hush, let me feel." He closed his eyes, not to shut out Louise, not to shut out Meg, but in order to see with his inner eye. "The dragons —I think—and a man, but more than a man—very tall and—" He opened his eyes, and pointed into the shadows where the trees crowded thickly together. "Look!"

Meg thought she saw a dim giant shape moving towards them, but before she could be sure, Fortinbras came galloping across the orchard, barking wildly. It was not his angry bark, but the loud announcing bark with which he greeted either of the Murry parents when they had been away. Then, with his heavy black tail lifted straight out behind him, his nose pointing and quivering, he stalked the length of the orchard, jumped the wall to the north pasture, and ran, still sniffing, to one of the big glacial rocks.

Charles Wallace, panting with effort, followed him.

"He's going to where my dragons were! Come on, Meg, maybe he's found fewmets!"

She hurried after boy and dog. "How would you know a dragon dropping? Fewmets probably look like bigger and better cow pies."

Charles Wallace was down on his hands and knees. "Look."

On the moss around the rock was a small drift of feathers. They did not look like bird feathers. They were extraordinarily soft and sparkling at the same time; and between the feathers were bits of glinting silver-gold, leaf-shaped scales which, Meg thought, might well belong to dragons.

"You see, Meg! They were here! My dragons were here!"

27

2 A Rip in the Galaxy

When Meg and Charles Wallace returned to the house, silently, each holding strange and new thoughts, evening was moving in with the wind. The twins were waiting for them, and wanted Charles Wallace to go out in the last of the light to play catch.

"It's too dark already," Charles Wallace said.

"We've got a few minutes. Come on, Charles. You may be bright, but you're slow at playing ball. I could pitch when I was six, and you can't even catch without fumbling."

Dennys patted Charles, a pat more like a whack. "He's improving. Come on, we've only got a few minutes."

Charles Wallace shook his head. He did not mention that he did not feel well; he just said, firmly, "Not tonight."

Meg left the twins still arguing with him, and went into the kitchen. Mrs. Murry was just coming in from the laboratory, and her mind was still on her work. She peered vaguely into the refrigerator.

Meg confronted her, "Mother, Charles Wallace thinks something is wrong with his mitochondria or farandolae or something."

Mrs. Murry shut the refrigerator door. "Sometimes Charles Wallace thinks too much."

"What does Dr. Colubra think? About this mitochondria bit?"

"That it's a possibility. Louise thinks the bad flu strain

this autumn, which has caused a lot of deaths, may not be flu at all, but mitochondritis."

"And that's what Charles maybe has?"

"I don't know, Meg. I'm trying to find out. When I know something, I will tell you. I've already said that. Meanwhile, let me alone."

Meg took a step backwards, sat down on one of the dining chairs. Her mother never talked in that cold, shutting-out way to her children. It must mean that she was very worried indeed.

Mrs. Murry turned towards Meg with an apologetic smile. "Sorry, Megatron. I didn't mean to be sharp. I'm in the difficult position of knowing more about the possible ailments of mitochondria than almost anybody else today. I didn't expect to be confronted with the results of my work quite so soon. And I still don't know enough to tell you— or Louise—anything definite. Meanwhile, there's no point in our getting all worried unless we know there's a real reason. Right now we'd better concentrate on Charles Wallace's problems at school."

"Is he well enough to go to school?"

"I think so. For now. I don't want to take him out until I have to."

"Why not?"

"He'd just have to go back eventually, Meg, and then things would be harder than ever. If he can just get through these first weeks—"

"Mother, nobody around here has ever known a six-year-old boy like Charles."

"He's extremely intelligent. But there was a day when

it wasn't unusual for a twelve- or thirteen-year-old to graduate from Harvard, or Oxford or Cambridge."

"It's unusual today. And you and Father can hardly send him to Harvard at six. Anyhow, it isn't just that he's intelligent. How does he know what we're thinking and feeling? I don't know how much you've told him, but he knows an awful lot about mitochondria and farandolae."

"I've told him a reasonable amount."

"He knows more than a reasonable amount. And he knows you're worried about him."

Mrs. Murry perched on one of the high stools by the kitchen counter which divided the work area from the rest of the bright, rambly dining and studying room. She sighed, "You're right, Meg. Charles Wallace not only has a good mind, he has extraordinary powers of intuition. If he can learn to discipline and channel them when he grows up—if he—" She broke off. "I have to think about getting dinner."

Meg knew when to stop pushing her mother. "I'll help. What're we having?" She did not mention Charles Wallace's dragons. She did not mention Louise the Larger's strange behavior, nor the shadow of whatever it was they had not quite seen.

"Oh, spaghetti's easy"—Mrs. Murry pushed a curl of dark red hair back from her forehead—"and good on an autumn night."

"And we've got all the tomatoes and peppers and stuff from the twins' garden. Mother, I love the twins even when they get in my hair, but Charles—"

30

"I know, Meg. You and Charles have always had a very special relationship."

"Mother, I can't stand what's happening to him at school."

"Neither can I, Meg."

"Then what are you doing about it?"

"We're trying to do nothing. It would be easy—for now—to take Charles out of school. We thought about that immediately, even before he— But Charles Wallace is going to have to live in a world made up of people who don't think at all in any of the ways that he does, and the sooner he starts learning to get along with them, the better. Neither you nor Charles has the ability to adapt that the twins do."

"Charles is a lot brighter than the twins."

"A life form which can't adapt doesn't last very long."

"I still don't like it."

"Neither do your father and I, Meg. Bear with us. Remember, you do have a tendency to rush in when the best thing to do is wait and be patient for a while."

"I'm not in the *least* patient."

"Is that for my information?" Mrs. Murry took tomatoes, onions, green and red peppers, garlic and leeks, out of the vegetable bin. Then, starting to slice onions into a large, black iron pot, she said thoughtfully, "You know, Meg, you went through a pretty rough time at school yourself."

"Not as bad as Charles. And I'm not as bright as Charles—except maybe in math."

"Possibly you're not—though you do tend to underestimate your own particular capacities. What I'm getting at is that you do seem, this year, to be finding school moderately bearable."

"Mr. Jenkins isn't there any more. And Calvin O'Keefe is. Calvin's important. He's the basketball star and president of the senior class and everything. Anybody Calvin likes is sort of protected by his—his aura."

"Why do you suppose Calvin likes you?"

"Not because of my beauty, that's for sure."

"But he does like you, doesn't he, Meg?"

"Well, yes, I guess so, but Calvin likes lots of people. And he could have any girl in school if he wanted to."

"But he chose you, didn't he?"

Meg could feel herself flushing. She put her hands up to her cheeks. "Well. Yes. But it's different. It's because of some of the things we've been through together. And we're friend-friends—I mean, we're not like most of the other kids."

"I'm glad you're friend-friends. I've become very fond of that skinny, carrot-headed young man."

Meg laughed. "I think Calvin confuses you with Pallas Athene. You're his absolute ideal. And he likes all of us. His own family's certainly a mess. I really think he likes me only because of our family."

Mrs. Murry sighed. "Stop being self-deprecating, Meg."

"Maybe at least I can learn to cook as well as you do. Did you know it was one of Calvin's brothers who beat Charles Wallace up today? I bet he's upset—I don't mean Whippy, he couldn't care less—Calvin. Somebody's bound to have told him."

"Do you want to call him?"

"Not me. Not Calvin. I just have to wait. Maybe he'll come over or something." She sighed. "I wish life didn't have to be so complicated. Do you suppose I'll ever be a double Ph.D. like you, Mother?"

Mrs. Murry looked up from slicing peppers, and laughed. "It's really not the answer to all problems. There are other solutions. At this point I'm more interested in knowing whether or not I've put too many red peppers in the spaghetti sauce; I've lost count."

They had just sat down to dinner when Mr. Murry phoned to tell them that he was going directly from Washington to Brookhaven for a week. Such trips were not unusual for either of their parents, but right now anything that took either her father or mother away struck Meg as sinister. Without much conviction she said, "I hope he has fun. He likes lots of the people there." But she felt a panicky dependence on having both her parents home at night. It wasn't only because of her fears for Charles Wallace; it was that suddenly the whole world was unsafe and uncertain. Several houses nearby had been broken into that autumn, and while nothing of great value had been taken, drawers had been emptied with casual maliciousness, food dumped on living-room floors, upholstery slashed. Even their safe little village was revealing itself to be unpredictable and irrational and precarious, and while Meg had already begun to understand this with her mind, she had never before felt it with the whole of herself. Now a cold awareness of the uncertainty of all life, no matter how careful the planning, hollowed emptily in the pit of her stomach. She swallowed.

Charles Wallace looked at her and said, unsmilingly, "The best laid plans of mice and men . . ."

"Gang aft agley," Sandy finished.

"Man proposes, God disposes," Dennys added, not to be outdone.

The twins held out their plates for more spaghetti, neither one ever having been known to lose his appetite. "Why does Father have to stay a whole week?" Sandy asked.

"It's his work, after all," Dennys said. "Mother, I think you could have put more hot peppers in the sauce."

"He's been away a lot this autumn. He ought to stay home with his family at least some of the time. I think the sauce is okay."

"Of course it's okay. I just like it a little hotter."

Meg was not thinking about spaghetti, although she was sprinkling Parmesan over hers. She wondered what their mother would say if Charles Wallace told her about his dragons. If there really were dragons, or a reasonable facsimile thereof, in the north pasture, oughtn't their parents to know?

Sandy said, "When I grow up I'm going to be a banker and make money. Someone in this family has to stay in the real world."

"Not that we don't think science is the real world, Mother," Dennys said, "but you and Father aren't practical scientists, you're theoretical scientists."

Mrs. Murry demurred, "I'm not wholly impractical, you know, Sandy, and neither is your father."

"Spending hours and hours peering into your micro-electron microscope, and listening to that micro-sonar whatsit isn't practical," Sandy announced.

"You just look at things nobody else can see," Dennys added, "and listen to things nobody else can hear, and think about them."

Meg defended her mother. "It would be a good idea if more people knew how to think. After Mother thinks about something long enough, then she puts it into practice. Or someone else does."

Charles Wallace cocked his head with a pleased look. "Does *practical* mean that something works out in practice?"

His mother nodded.

"So it doesn't matter if Mother sits and thinks. Or if Father spends weeks over one equation. Even if he writes it on the tablecloth. His equations are practical if someone else makes them work out in practice." He reached in his pocket, as though in answer to Meg's thoughts about the dragons, and drew out a feather, not a bird feather, but a strange glitter catching the light. "All right, my practical brothers, what is this?"

Sandy, sitting next to Charles Wallace, bent over the dragon feather. "A feather."

Dennys got up and went around the table so that he could see. "Let me—"

Charles Wallace held the feather between them. "What kind is it?"

"Hey, this is most peculiar!" Sandy touched the base of the feather. "I don't think it's from a bird."

35

"Why not?" Charles Wallace asked.

"The rachis isn't right."

"The what?" Meg asked.

"The rachis. Sort of part of the quill. The rachis should be hollow, and this is solid, and seems to be metallic. Hey, Charles, where'd you get this thing?"

Charles Wallace handed the feather to his mother. She looked at it carefully. "Sandy's right. The rachis isn't like a bird's."

Dennys said, "Then what—"

Charles Wallace retrieved the feather and put it back in his pocket. "It was on the ground by the big rocks in the north pasture. Not just this one feather. Quite a few others."

Meg suppressed a slightly hysterical giggle. "Charles and I think it may be fewmets."

Sandy turned to her with injured dignity. "Fewmets are dragon droppings."

Dennys said, "Don't be silly." Then, "Do you know what it is, Mother?"

She shook her head. "What do you think it is, Charles?"

Charles Wallace, as he occasionally did, retreated into himself. When Meg had decided he wasn't going to answer at all, he said, "It's something that's not in Sandy's and Dennys's practical world. When I find out more, I'll tell you." He sounded very like their mother.

"Okay, then." Dennys had lost interest. He returned to his chair. "Did Father tell you why he has to go rushing off to Brookhaven, or is it another of those top-secret classified things?"

Mrs. Murry looked down at the checked tablecloth, and at the remains of an equation which had not come out in the wash; doodling equations on anything available was a habit of which she could not break her husband. "It's not really secret. There've been several bits about it in the papers recently."

"About what?" Sandy asked.

"There's been an unexplainable phenomenon, not in our part of the galaxy, but far across it, and in several other galaxies—well, the easiest way to explain it is that our new supersensitive sonic instruments have been picking up strange sounds, sounds which aren't on any normal register, but much higher. After such a sound—a cosmic scream, the *Times* rather sensationally called it—there appears to be a small rip in the galaxy."

"What does that mean?" Dennys asked.

"It seems to mean that several stars have vanished."

"Vanished where?"

"That's the odd part. Vanished. Completely. Where the stars were there is, as far as our instruments can detect, nothing. Your father was out in California several weeks ago, you remember, at Mount Palomar."

"But things can't just vanish," Sandy said. "We had it in school—the balance of matter."

Their mother added, very quietly, "It seems to be getting unbalanced."

"You mean like the ecology?"

"No. I mean that matter actually seems to be being annihilated."

Dennys said flatly, "But that's impossible."

"$E = MC^2$," Sandy said. "Matter can be converted into energy, and energy into matter. You have to have one or the other."

Mrs. Murry said, "Thus far, Einstein's law has never been disproved. But it's coming into question."

"Nothingness—" Dennys said. "That's impossible."

"One would hope so."

"And that's what Father's going off about?"

"Yes, to consult with several other scientists, Shasti from India, Shen Shu from China—you've heard of them."

Outside the dining-room windows came a sudden brilliant flash of light, followed by a loud clap of thunder. The windows rattled. The kitchen door burst open. Everybody jumped.

Meg sprang up, crying nervously, "Oh, Mother—"

"Sit down, Meg. You've heard thunder before."

"You're sure it's not one of those cosmic things?"

Sandy shut the door.

Mrs. Murry was calmly reassuring. "Positive. They're completely inaudible to human ears." Lightning flashed again. Thunder boomed. "As a matter of fact, there are only two instruments in the world delicate enough to pick up the sound, which is incredibly high-pitched. It's perfectly possible that it's been going on for billennia, and only now are our instruments capable of recording it."

"Birds can hear sounds way above our normal pitch," Sandy said, "I mean, way up the scale, that we can't hear at all."

"Birds can't hear this."

Dennys said, "I wonder if snakes can hear as high a pitch as birds?"

"Snakes don't have ears," Sandy contradicted.

"So? They feel vibrations and sound waves. I think Louise hears all kinds of things out of human range. What's for dessert?"

Meg's voice was still tense. "We don't usually have thunderstorms in October."

"Please calm down, Meg." Mrs. Murry started clearing the table. "If you'll stop and think, you'll remember that we've had an unseasonable storm for every month in the year."

Sandy said, "Why does Meg always exaggerate everything? Why does she have to be so cosmic? What's for dessert?"

"I don't—" Meg started defensively, then jumped as the rain began to pelt against the windows.

"There's some ice cream in the freezer," Mrs. Murry said. "Sorry, I haven't been thinking about desserts."

"Meg's supposed to make desserts," Dennys said. "Not that we expect pies or anything, Meg, but even you can't go too wrong with Jello."

Charles Wallace caught Meg's eye, and she closed her mouth. He put his hand in the pocket of his robe again, though this time he did not produce the feather, and gave her a small, private smile. He may have been thinking about his dragons, but he had also been listening carefully, both to the conversation and to the storm, his fair head tilted slightly to one side. "This ripping in the galaxy,

Mother—does it have any effect on our own solar system?"

"That," Mrs. Murry replied, "is what we would all like to know."

Sandy brushed this aside impatiently. "It's all much too complicated for me. I'm sure banking is a lot simpler."

"And more lucrative," Dennys added.

The windows shook in the wind. The twins looked through the darkness at the slashing rain.

"It's a good thing we brought in so much stuff from the garden before dinner."

"This is almost hail."

Meg asked nervously, "Is it dangerous, this—this ripping in the sky, or whatever it is?"

"Meg, we really know nothing about it. It may have been going on all along, and we only now have the instruments to record it."

"Like farandolae," Charles Wallace said. "We tend to think things are new because we've just discovered them."

"But is it dangerous?" Meg repeated.

"Meg, we don't know enough about it yet. That's why it's important that your father and some of the other physicists get together at once."

"But it could be dangerous?"

"Anything can be dangerous."

Meg looked down at the remains of her dinner. Dragons and rips in the sky. Louise and Fortinbras greeting something large and strange. Charles Wallace pale and listless. She did not like any of it. "I'll do the dishes," she told her mother.

They cleaned up the kitchen in silence. Mrs. Murry had

sent the reluctant twins to practice for the school orchestra, Dennys on the flute, which he played well, accompanied by Sandy, less skillfully, on the piano. But it was a pleasant, familiar noise, and Meg relaxed into it. When the dishwasher was humming, the pots and pans polished and hung on their hooks, she went up to her attic bedroom to do her homework. This room was supposed to be her own, private place, and it would have been perfect except for the fact that it was seldom really private: the twins kept their electric trains in the big, open section of the attic; the ping-pong table was there, and anything anybody didn't want around downstairs but didn't want to throw away. Although Meg's room was at the far end of the attic, it was easily available to the twins when they needed help with their math homework. And Charles Wallace always knew, without being told, when she was troubled, and would come up to the attic to sit on the foot of her bed. The only time she didn't want Charles Wallace was when he himself was what was troubling her. She did not want him now.

Rain was still spattering against her window, but with diminishing force. The wind was swinging around from the south to the west; the storm was passing and the temperature falling. Her room was cold, but she did not plug in the little electric heater her parents had given her to supplement the inadequate heat which came up the attic stairs. Instead, she shoved her books aside and tiptoed back downstairs, stepping carefully over the seventh stair, which not only creaked but sometimes gave off a report like a shot.

The twins were still practicing. Her mother was in the

living room, in front of the fire, reading to Charles Wallace, not from books about trains, or animals, which the twins had liked at that age, but from a scientific magazine, an article called "The Polarizabilities and Hyperpolarizabilities of Small Molecules," by the theoretical chemist, Peter Liebmann.

—Ouch, Meg thought ruefully. —This kind of thing is Charles Wallace's bedtime reading and our parents expect him to go to first grade and not get into trouble?

Charles Wallace lay on the floor in front of the fire, staring into the flames, half listening, half brooding, his head as usual pillowed on Fortinbras's comfortable bulk. Meg would have liked to take Fort with her, but that would mean letting the family know she was going out. She hurried as quickly and silently as possible through the kitchen and out into the pantry. As she pulled the kitchen door closed behind her, slowly, carefully, so nobody would hear, the pantry door flew open with a bang, and the door to her mother's lab, on the left, slammed shut in a gust of wind.

She stopped, listened, waited for one of the twins to open the kitchen door and see what was going on. But nothing happened except that the wind blew wildly through the pantry. She shivered, and grabbed the first rain clothes that came to hand, a big black rubber poncho that belonged to the twins and had done double duty as a ground cloth for a tent; and Charles Wallace's yellow sou'wester. Then she took the big flashlight from the hook, shut the pantry door firmly behind her, and ran across the lawn, tripping over the croquet wicket. Limping, she crossed the patch of dandelion, burdock, and milkweed that was growing up in the opening the twins had cut in the barberry fence. Once she was in the vegetable garden she hoped that she would be invisible to anybody chancing to look out a window. She could imagine Sandy's or Dennys's reaction if they asked her where she was going and she told them she was looking for dragons.

Why, in fact, had she come out? And what was she looking for? Was it dragons? Fortinbras and Louise both had seen—and not been afraid of—something, something which had left the feathers and scales. And that something—or somethings—was likely to be uncomfortable in the wet pasture. If it—or they—came to seek shelter in the house, she wanted to be prepared.

Not only for dragons, in which she did not quite believe, despite her faith in Charles Wallace and the feather with the peculiar rachis, but also for Louise the Larger. The twins insisted that Louise was an unusual snake, but this afternoon was the first time Meg had seen any signs that Louise was anything more than a contented, common garden-variety snake.

Meg checked the shadows on the wall, but there was no sign of Louise, so she lingered, not at all anxious to cross the apple orchard and go into the north pasture to the two glacial rocks. For a few minutes she would stay in the homely garden, and gather her courage, and be safe from discovery: the twins were hardly likely to come out after dark in the cold and wet, to admire the last few cabbages, or the vine which had borne their prize cucumber, the size of a vegetable marrow.

The garden was bordered on the east by two rows of

43

sunflowers which stood with their heavy, fringed heads bowed over so that they looked like a huddle of witches; Meg glanced at them nervously; raindrops dripped from their faces with melancholy unconcern, but no longer from the sky. There was a hint of light from the full moon behind the thinning clouds, turning all the vegetables into beings strange and unreal. The gaping rows where once beans had stood, and lettuce, and peas, had a forlorn look; there was an air of sadness and confusion about the carefully planned pattern.

"Like everything else"—Meg spoke to the few remaining cauliflower heads—"it's falling apart. It's not right in the United States of America that a little kid shouldn't be safe in school."

She moved slowly along the orchard wall. The cidery smell of fallen apples was cut by the wind which had completely changed course and was now streaming across the garden from the northwest, sharp and glittery with frost. She saw a shadow move on the wall and jumped back: Louise the Larger, it must be Louise, and Meg could not climb that wall or cross the orchard to the north pasture until she was sure that neither Louise nor the not-quite-seen shape was lurking there waiting to pounce on her. Her legs felt watery, so she sat on a large, squat pumpkin to wait. The cold wind brushed her cheek; corn tassels hished like ocean waves. She looked warily about. She was seeing, she realized, through lenses streaked and spattered by raindrops blowing from sunflowers and corn, so she took off her spectacles, felt under the poncho for her kilt, and wiped them. Better, though the world was still a little wavery, as though seen under water.

She listened; listened. In the orchard she heard the soft plomp of falling apples; wind shaking the trees; branches rustling. She peered through the darkness. Something was moving, coming closer—

Snakes never come out in the cold and dark, she knew that. Nevertheless—

Louise—

Yes, it was the big snake. She emerged from the rocks of the stone wall, slowly, warily, watchfully. Meg's heart was thumping, although Louise was not threatening. At least, Louise was not threatening *her*. But Louise was waiting, and this time there was no welcome in the waiting. Meg looked in fascination as the head of the snake slowly weaved back and forth, then quivered in recognition.

Behind Meg a voice came. "Margaret."

She whirled around.

It was Mr. Jenkins. She looked at him in complete bewilderment.

He said, "Your little brother thought I might find you here, Margaret."

Yes, Charles would guess, would know where she was. But why would Mr. Jenkins have been speaking to Charles Wallace? The principal had never been to the Murrys' house, or any parents', for that matter. All confrontations were in the safe anonymity of his office. Why would he come through the wet grass and the still-dripping garden to look for her instead of sending one of the twins?

He said, "I wanted to come find you myself, Margaret, because I feel that I owe you an apology for my sharpness with you last week when you came to see me." He held out a hand, pale in the moonlight wavering behind the clouds.

In utter confusion she reached out to take his hand, and as she did so, Louise rose up on the wall behind her, hissing and making a strange, warning clacking. Meg turned to see the snake, looking as large and hooded as a cobra, hissing angrily at Mr. Jenkins, raising her large dark coils to strike.

Mr. Jenkins screamed, in a way that she had never known a man could scream, a high, piercing screech.

Then he rose up into the night like a great, flapping bird, flew, screaming across the sky, became a rent, an emptiness, a slash of nothingness—

Meg found that she, too, was screaming.

It could not have happened.

There was no one, no thing there.

She thought she saw Louise slithering back through a dark recess in the stone wall, disappearing—

It was impossible.

Her mind had snapped. It was some kind of hallucination caused by the weather, by her anxiety, by the state of the world—

A thick, ugly smell, like spoiled cabbage, like flower stalks left too long in water, rose like a miasma from the place where Mr. Jenkins had been—

But he could not have been there—

She screamed again, in uncontrollable panic, as a tall shape hurtled towards her.

Calvin. Calvin O'Keefe.

She burst into hysterical tears of relief.

He vaulted over the wall to her, his strong, thin arms tight around her, holding her. "Meg. Meg, what is it?"

She could not control her terrified sobbing.

"Meg, what's the matter? What's happened?" He shook her, urgently.

Gasping, she tried to tell him. "I know it sounds incredible—" she finished. She was still trembling violently, her heart racing. When he did not speak, but continued soothingly to pat her back, she said, through a few final, hiccuping sobs, "Oh, Calvin, I wish I *had* imagined it. Do you think—do you think maybe I did?"

"I don't know," Calvin said flatly. He continued to hold her strongly, comfortingly.

Now that Calvin was here, would take over, she was able to manage a slightly hysterical giggle. "Mr. Jenkins always said I have too much imagination—but it's never been *that* kind of imagination. I've never hallucinated or anything, have I?"

"No," he replied firmly. "You have not. What's that awful stench?"

"I don't know. It's not nearly as bad now as it was just before you came."

"It makes silage smell like roses. Yukh."

"Calvin—Louise the Larger—it's not the first time today Louise has done something peculiar."

"What?"

She told him about Louise that afternoon. "But she wasn't attacking or anything then, she was still friendly.

47

She's always been a friendly snake." She let her breath out in a long, quavering sigh. "Cal, let me have your handkerchief, please. My glasses are filthy and I can't see a thing, and right now I'd like to be able to see what's going on."

"My handkerchief is filthy." But Calvin fished in his pockets.

"It's better than a kilt." Meg spat on her glasses and wiped them. Without their aid she could see no more of the older boy than a vague blur, so she made bold to say, "Oh, Cal, I was hoping you might come over tonight anyhow."

"I'm surprised you're even willing to speak to me. I came over to apologize for what my brother did to Charles Wallace."

Meg adjusted her spectacles with her usual rough shove up the nose, just as a shaft of moonlight broke through the clouds and illuminated Calvin's troubled expression. She returned his handkerchief. "It wasn't your fault." Then— "I must have had a mental aberration or something, about Louise and Mr. Jenkins, mustn't I?"

"I don't know, Meg. You've never had a mental aberration before, have you?"

"Not that I know of."

"Fewmets to Mr. Jenkins, anyhow."

She almost shouted, "What did you say!"

"Fewmets to Mr. Jenkins. Fewmets is my new swear word. I'm tired of all the old ones. Fewmets are dragon droppings, and—"

"I know fewmets are dragon droppings! What I want to

know is why you picked on fewmets, of all things?"

"It seemed quite a reasonable choice to me."

Suddenly she was shaking again. "Calvin—please—don't —it's too serious."

He dropped his bantering tone. "Okay, Meg, what's up about fewmets?"

"Oh, Cal, I was so sort of shook about the Mr. Jenkins thing I almost forgot about the dragons."

"The what?"

She told him, all about Charles Wallace and his dragons, "and he's never hallucinated before, either." She told him again about Louise greeting the shadow of something they had not quite seen, "but it certainly wasn't Mr. Jenkins. Louise wasn't in the least friendly about Mr. Jenkins."

"It's wild," Calvin said, "absolutely wild."

"But we did see fewmets, Calvin—or something, more like feathers, really, but not like real feathers. Charles Wallace took one home—there was a whole pile of them— these sort of feathers, and dragon scales, by the biggest rock in the north pasture."

Calvin sprang to his feet. "Let's go, then! Bring your flashlight."

It was possible now for her to cross the orchard and go into the pasture with Calvin to take the lead. Uppermost in Meg's mind, superseding fear, was the need to prove that she and Charles Wallace weren't just making something up, that the wild tales she had told Calvin were real—not Mr. Jenkins turning into a flying emptiness in the sky, she did not want that to be real, but the dragons. For if nothing

49

that had happened touched on reality, then she was going out of her mind.

When they reached the pasture, Calvin took the light from her. "I'll go ahead a bit."

But Meg followed close on his heels. She thought she could sense disbelief as he swept the arc of light around the base of the rock. The beam came to rest in a small circle, and in the center of the circle shone something gold and glittering.

"Phew—" Calvin said.

Meg giggled with relief and tension. "Don't you mean fewmets? Has anybody ever seen a fewmet?"

Calvin was down on hands and knees, running his fingers through the little pile of feathers and scales. "Okay, okay, this is most peculiar. But what left it? After all, a gang of dragons just doesn't disappear."

"A drive of dragons," Meg corrected, automatically. "Do you really think it's dragons?"

Calvin did not answer. He asked, "Did you tell your mother?"

"Charles Wallace showed the feather to the twins during dinner, and Mother saw it, too. The twins said it wasn't a bird's feather because the rachis isn't right, and then the conversation got shifted. I think Charles shifted it on purpose."

"How is he?" Calvin asked. "How badly did Whippy hurt him?"

"He's been hurt worse. Mother put compresses on his eye, and it's turning black and blue. But that's about all."

She was not ready, yet, to mention his pallor, or shortness of wind. "You'd think we lived in the roughest section of an inner city or something, instead of way out in the peaceful country. There isn't a day he doesn't get shoved around by one of the bigger kids—it's not only Whippy. Cal, why is it that my parents know all about physics and biology and stuff, and nothing about keeping their son from being mugged?"

Calvin pulled himself up onto the smaller of the two stones. "If it's any consolation to you, Meg, I doubt if my parents know the difference between physics and biology. Maybe Charles would be better off in a city school, where there're lots of different kinds of kids, white, black, yellow, Spanish-speaking, rich, poor. Maybe he wouldn't stand out as being so different if there were other different people, too. Here—well, everybody's sort of alike. People're kind of proud of having your parents live here, and pally with the President and all, but you Murrys certainly aren't like anybody else."

"You've managed."

"Same way the twins have. Playing by the laws of the jungle. You know that. Anyhow, my parents and grand-parents were born right here in the village, and so were my great-grandparents. The O'Keefes may be shiftless, but at least they're not newcomers." His voice deepened with an old sadness.

"Oh, Cal—"

He shrugged his dark mood aside. "I think maybe we'd better go talk to your mother."

"Not yet." Charles Wallace's voice came from behind them. "She's got enough worries. Let's wait till the dragons come back."

Meg jumped. "Charles! Why aren't you in bed? Does Mother know you're out?"

"I was in bed. Mother doesn't know I'm out. Obviously."

Meg was near tears of exhaustion. "Nothing is obvious any more." Then, in her big-sister tone of voice: "You shouldn't be out this late."

"What happened?"

"What do you mean?"

"Meg, I came out because something frightened you." He sighed, a strangely tired and ancient sigh from so small a boy. "I was almost asleep and I felt you screaming."

"I don't want to tell you about it. I don't want it to have happened. Where's Fortinbras?"

"I left him at home and told him not to let on that I wasn't sound asleep in bed. I didn't want him tangling with dragons. Meg, what happened? You've got to tell me."

Meg said, "Okay, Charles, I don't doubt your dragons any more. No dragons could be more incredible than Mr. Jenkins coming to look for me in the garden, and then turning into a—a great shrieking bird of nothingness." She spoke quickly, because what she was saying sounded so absurd.

Charles Wallace did not laugh. He opened his mouth to speak, then swung around. "Who's here?"

"Nobody," Calvin said. "Meg and me. You." But he jumped down from the rock.

"There's somebody else. Near."

Meg moved closer to Calvin. Her heart, it seemed, stopped beating.

"Hush," Charles Wallace said, though they had not spoken. He listened with lifted head, like Fortinbras catching a scent.

To the right of the pasture was a woods, a small forest of oak, maple, beech, stripped of all but a few brittle leaves, backed by the dark winter richness of assorted spruce and pine. The ground, which the moonlight did not reach, was covered with fallen damp leaves and pine needles which would silence footsteps. Then they heard the sharp crack of a breaking twig.

Meg and Calvin, straining to peer through the trees, saw nothing.

Then Charles Wallace cried, "My dragons!"

They turned around, and they saw, there by the great rock—

wings, it seemed like hundreds of wings, spreading, folding, stretching—

and eyes

how many eyes can a drive of dragons have?

and small jets of flame

Suddenly a voice called to them from the direction of the woods, "Do not be afraid!"

3 The Man in the Night

A huge dark form strode swiftly through the woods and into the pasture; it reached them in a few strides, and then stood very still, so that the folds of the long robe seemed chiseled out of granite.

"Do not be afraid," he repeated. "He won't hurt you."

He?

Yes. Charles Wallace's drive of dragons was a single creature, although Meg was not at all surprised that Charles Wallace had confused this fierce, wild being with dragons. She had the feeling that she never saw all of it at once, and which of all the eyes could she meet? merry eyes, wise eyes, ferocious eyes, kitten eyes, dragon eyes, opening and closing, looking at her, looking at Charles Wallace and Calvin and the strange tall man. And wings, wings in constant motion, covering and uncovering the eyes. When the wings were spread out they had a span of at least ten feet, and when they were all folded in, the creature resembled a misty, feathery sphere. Little spurts of flame and smoke spouted up between the wings; it could certainly start a grass fire if it weren't careful. Meg did not wonder that Charles Wallace had not approached it.

Again the tall stranger reassured them. "He won't hurt you." The stranger was dark, dark as night and tall as a tree, and there was something in the repose of his body, the quiet of his voice, which drove away fear.

Charles Wallace stepped towards him. "Who are you?"

"A Teacher."

Charles Wallace's sigh was longing. "I wish you were *my* teacher."

"I am." The cello-like voice was calm, slightly amused.

Charles Wallace advanced another step. "And my dragons?"

The tall man—the Teacher—held out his hand in the direction of the wild creature, which seemed to gather itself together, to rise up, to give a great, courteous bow to all of them.

The Teacher said, "His name is Proginoskes."

Charles Wallace said, "He?"

"Yes."

"He's not dragons?"

"He is a cherubim."

"What!?"

"A cherubim."

Flame spurted skywards in indignation at the doubt in the atmosphere. Great wings raised and spread and the children were looked at by a great many eyes. When the wild thing spoke, it was not in vocal words, but directly into their minds.

"I suppose you think I ought to be a golden-haired baby-face with no body and two useless little wings?"

Charles Wallace stared at the great creature. "It might be simpler if you were."

Meg pulled her poncho closer about her, for protection in case the cherubim spouted fire in her direction.

"It is a constant amazement to me," the cherubim thought at them, "that so many earthling artists paint cherubim to resemble baby pigs."

Calvin made a sound which, if he had been less astonished, would have been a laugh. "But cherubim is plural."

The fire-spouting beast returned, "I am practically plural. The little boy thought I was a drive of dragons, didn't he? I am certainly not a cherub. I am a singular cherubim."

"What are you doing here?" Charles Wallace asked.

"I was sent."

"Sent?"

"To be in your class. I don't know what I've done to be assigned to a class with such immature earthlings. I have a hard enough job as it is. I really don't fancy coming back to school at all at my age."

"How old are you?" Meg held her poncho out wide, ready to use it as a shield.

"Age, for cherubim, is immaterial. It's only for time-bound creatures that age even exists. I am, in cherubic terms, still a child, and that is all you need to know. It's very rude to ask questions about age." Two of the wings crossed and uncrossed. The message had been rueful, rather than annoyed.

Charles Wallace spoke to the tall man. "You are my teacher, and his teacher, too?"

"I am."

Charles Wallace looked up at the strange dark face which was stern and gentle at the same time. "It's too good

56

to be true. I think I must be having a dream. I wish I'd just go on dreaming and not wake up."

"What is real?" The Teacher stretched out an arm, and gently touched the bruise on Charles Wallace's cheek, the puffed and discolored flesh under his eye. "You are awake."

"Or if you're asleep," Meg said, "we're all having the same dream. Aren't we, Calvin?"

"The thing that makes me think we're awake is that if I were to dream about a cherubim, it wouldn't look like that—that—"

Several very blue, long-lashed eyes looked directly at Calvin. "Proginoskes, as the Teacher told you. Proginoskes. And don't get any ideas about calling me Cherry, or Cheery, or Bimmy."

"It would be easier," Charles Wallace said.

But the creature repeated firmly, "Proginoskes."

Out of the dark form of the Teacher came a deep, gentle rumbling of amusement, a rumbling which expanded and rose and bubbled into a great laugh. "All right, then, my children. Are you ready to start—we will call it, for want of a better word in your language, school—are you ready to start school?"

Charles Wallace, a small and rather ludicrous figure in the yellow slicker he had pulled on over his pajamas, looked up at the oak-tree height and strength of the Teacher. "The sooner the better. Time's running out."

"Hey, wait a minute," Calvin objected. "What are you going to do with Charles? You and the—the cherubim can't take him off without consulting his parents."

"What makes you think I'm planning to?" The Teacher

57

gave an easy little jump, and there he was, comfortably sitting on the tallest of the glacial rocks as though it were a stool, his arms loosely about his knees, the folds of his robe blending with the moonlit stone. "And I came not only to call Charles Wallace. I came to call all three of you."

Meg looked startled. "All of us? But——"

"You may address me as Blajeny," the Teacher said.

Charles Wallace asked, "Mr. Blajeny? Dr. Blajeny? Sir Blajeny?"

"Blajeny is enough. That is all of my name you need to know. Are you ready?"

Meg still looked astonished. "Calvin and me, too?"

"Yes."

"But——" As always when she felt unsure, Meg was argumentative. "Calvin doesn't need—he's the best student in school, and the best athlete, he's important and everything. And I'm getting along, now. It's Charles who's the trouble —you can see for yourself. School, ordinary school, is just not going to work out for him."

Blajeny's voice was cool. "That is hardly my problem."

"Then why are you here?" That Blajeny might have been sent solely to help her brother did not seem at all astonishing to Meg.

Again came the rumble that bubbled up into a laugh. "My dears, you must not take yourselves so seriously. Why should school be easy for Charles Wallace?"

"It shouldn't be *this* bad. This is the United States of America. They'll hurt him if somebody doesn't do something."

"He will have to learn to defend himself."

Charles Wallace, looking very small and defenseless, spoke quietly. "The Teacher is right. It's a question of learning to adapt, and nobody can do that for me. If everybody will leave me alone, and stop trying to help me, I'll learn, eventually, how not to be conspicuous. I can assure you I haven't mentioned mitochondria and farandolae lately."

The Teacher nodded grave approval.

Charles Wallace moved closer to him. "I'm very glad you haven't come because I'm making such a mess of school. But—Blajeny—if you haven't come because of that, then why are you here?"

"I have come not so much to offer you my help as to ask for yours."

"Ours?" Meg asked.

Charles Wallace looked up at the Teacher. "I'm not much of a help to anybody right now. It isn't just that I'm not getting along at school—"

"Yes," Blajeny said. "I know of the other problem. Nevertheless you are called, and anybody who is invited to study with one of the Teachers is called because he is needed. You have talents we cannot afford to lose."

"Then—"

"We must find out what is making you ill and, if possible, make you well again."

"If possible?" Meg asked anxiously.

Calvin asked sharply, "Charles? Ill? What's wrong? What's the matter with Charles?"

"Look at him," Meg said in a low voice. "Look how

pale he is. And he has trouble breathing. He got out of breath just walking across the orchard." She turned to the Teacher. "Oh, please, please, Blajeny, can you help?"

Blajeny looked down at her, darkly, quietly. "I think, my child, that it is you who must help."

"Me?"

"Yes."

"You know I'd do anything in the world to help Charles." Calvin looked questioningly at the Teacher.

"Yes, Calvin, you too."

"How? How can we help?"

"You will learn as the lessons progress."

Calvin asked, "Where are we going to have these lessons, then? Where's your school?"

Blajeny jumped lightly down from the rock. Despite his height and girth he moved, Meg thought, as though he were used to a heavier gravity than earth's. He strode lightly halfway across the pasture to where there was a large, flat rock where the children often went with their parents to watch the stars. He dropped down onto the rock and lay stretched out on his back, gesturing to the others to join him. Meg lay beside him, with Calvin on her other side, so that she felt protected, not only from the cold night wind but from the cherubim, who had reached the rock with the beat of a wing and assorted himself into an assemblage of wings and eyes and puffs of smoke at a discreet distance from Charles Wallace, who was on Blajeny's other side.

"It's all right, dragons," Charles Wallace said. "I'm not afraid of you."

The cherubim rearranged his wings. "Proginoskes, please."

Blajeny looked up at the sky, raised his arm, and made a wide, embracing gesture. The clouds had almost dispersed; only a few rapidly flying streamers veiled the stars, which blazed with the fierce brilliance of the rapidly plummeting mercury. The Teacher's sweeping motion indicated the entire sparkling stretch of sky. Then he sat up and folded his arms across his chest, and his strange luminous eyes turned inwards, so that he was looking not at the stars nor at the children but into some deep, dark place far within himself, and then further. He sat there, moving in, in, deeper and deeper, for time out of time. Then the focus of his eyes returned to the children, and he gave his radiant smile and answered Calvin's question as though not a moment had passed.

"Where is my school? Here, there, everywhere. In the schoolyard during first-grade recess. With the cherubim and seraphim. Among the farandolae."

Charles Wallace exclaimed, "My mother's isolated the farandolae!"

"So she has."

"Blajeny, do you know if something's wrong with my farandolae and mitochondria?"

Blajeny replied quietly, "Your mother and Dr. Colubra are trying to find that out."

"Well, then, what do we do now?"

"Go home to bed."

"But school—"

"You will all go to school as usual in the morning."

It was total anticlimax. "But *your* school—" Meg cried in disappointment. She had hoped that Charles Wallace would never have to enter the old red school building again, that Blajeny would take over, make everything all right . . .

"My children," Blajeny said gravely, "my school building is the entire cosmos. Before your time with me is over, I may have to take you great distances, and to very strange places."

"Are we your whole class?" Calvin asked. "Meg and Charles Wallace and me?"

Proginoskes let out a puff of huffy smoke.

"Sorry—and the cherubim."

Blajeny said, "Wait. You will know when the time comes."

"And why on earth is one of our classmates a cherubim?" Meg said. "Sorry, Proginoskes, but it does seem very insulting to *you* to have to be with mortals like us."

Proginoskes batted several eyes in apology. "I didn't mean what I said about immature earthlings. If we have been sent to the same Teacher, then we have things to learn from each other. A cherubim is not a *higher* order than earthlings, you know, just different."

Blajeny nodded. "Yes. You have much to learn from each other. Meanwhile, I will give each of you assignments. Charles Wallace, can you guess what yours is?"

"To learn to adapt."

"I don't want you to change!" Meg cried.

"Neither do I," Blajeny replied. "Charles Wallace's

62

problem is to learn to adapt while remaining wholly himself."

"What's my assignment, Blajeny?" Meg asked.

The Teacher frowned briefly, in thought. Then, "I am trying to put it into earth terms, terms which you will understand. You must pass three tests, or trials. You must start immediately on the first one."

"What is it?"

"Part of the trial is that you must discover for yourself what it is."

"But how?"

"That I cannot tell you. But you will not be alone. Proginoskes is to work with you. You will be what I think you would call partners. Together you must pass the three tests."

"But suppose we fail?"

Proginoskes flung several wings over his eyes in horror at the thought.

Blajeny said quietly, "It is a possibility, but I would prefer you not to suppose any such thing. Remember that these three trials will be nothing you could imagine or expect right now."

"But Blajeny—I can hardly take a cherubim to school with me!"

Blajeny looked affectionately at the great creature, whose wings were still folded protectingly about himself. "That is for the two of you to decide. He is not always visible, you know. Myself, I find him a little simpler when he's just a wind or a flame, but he was convinced he'd be more reassuring to earthlings if he enfleshed himself."

Charles Wallace reached out and slipped his hand into

the Teacher's. "If I could take him, just this way, looking like a drive of dragons, into the schoolyard with me, I bet I wouldn't have any trouble."

Meg said, "Didn't you tell me you were supposed to bring a pet to school tomorrow?"

Charles Wallace laughed. "We *may* bring a small pet tomorrow to share with the class."

Proginoskes peered under one wing. "I am not a joking matter."

"Oh, Progo," Meg assured him. "It's only whistling in the dark."

Charles Wallace, still holding the Teacher's hand, asked him, "Will you come home with us now and meet my mother?"

"Not tonight, Charles, it is very late for you to be up, and who knows what tomorrow will bring?"

"Don't *you* know?"

"I am only a Teacher, and I would not arrange the future ahead of time if I could. Come, I will walk part of the way back to the house with you."

Meg asked, "What about Progo—Proginoskes?"

The cherubim replied, "If it is not the time for Blajeny to meet your family, it is hardly the time for me. I am quite comfortable here. Perhaps you could come meet me early tomorrow morning, and we can compare our night thoughts."

"Well—okay. I guess that's best. Good night, then."

"Good night, Megling." He waved a wing at her, then folded himself up into a great puff. No eyes showed, no flame, no smoke.

THE MAN IN THE NIGHT

Meg shivered.

Blajeny asked, "Are you cold?"

She shivered again. "That thunderstorm before dinner—I suppose it was caused by a cold front meeting a warm front, but it did seem awfully cosmic. I never expected to meet a cherubim . . ."

"Blajeny," Calvin said, "you haven't given me an assignment."

"No, my son. There is work for you, difficult work, and dangerous, but I cannot tell you yet what it is. Your assignment is to wait, without question. Please come to the Murrys' house after school tomorrow—you are free to do that?"

"Oh, sure," Calvin said. "I can skip my after-school stuff for once."

"Good. Until then. Now, let us go."

Charles Wallace led the way, with Meg and Calvin close behind. The wind was blowing out of the northwest, colder, it seemed, with each gust. When they reached the stone wall to the apple orchard, the moon was shining clearly, with that extraordinary brightness which makes light and dark acute and separate. Some apples still clung to their branches; a few as dark as Blajeny, others shining with a silvery light, almost as though they were illuminated from within.

On top of the pale stones of the wall lay a dark shadow, which was moving slowly, sinuously. It rose up, carefully uncoiling, seeming to spread a hood as it loomed over them. Its forked tongue flickered, catching the light, and a hissing issued from its mouth.

Louise.

But this was not the threatening Louise who had hissed and clacked at the impossible Mr. Jenkins; this was the Louise Meg and Charles Wallace had seen that afternoon, the Louise who had been waiting to greet the unknown shadow—the shadow who, Meg suddenly understood, must have been Blajeny.

Nevertheless, she pressed closer to Calvin; she had never felt very secure around Louise, and the snake's strange behavior that afternoon and evening made her seem even more alien than when she was only the twins' pet.

Now Louise was weaving slowly back and forth in a gentle rhythm, almost as though she were making a serpentine version of a deep curtsy; and the sibilant sound was a gentle, treble fluting.

Blajeny bowed to the snake.

Louise most definitely returned the bow.

Blajeny explained gravely, "She is a colleague of mine."

"But—but—hey, now," Calvin sputtered, "wait a minute—"

"She is a Teacher. That is why she is so fond of the two boys—Sandy and Dennys. One day they will be Teachers, too."

Meg said, "They're going to be successful businessmen and support the rest of us in the way to which we are not accustomed."

Blajeny waved this aside. "They will be Teachers. It is a High Calling, and you must not be distressed that it is not yours. You, too, have a Work."

Louise, with a last burst of her tiny, strange melody,

dropped back to the wall and disappeared among the stones.

"Perhaps we're dreaming after all," Calvin said, wonderingly.

"What is real?" the Teacher asked again. "I will say good night to you now."

Charles Wallace was reluctant to leave. "We won't wake up in the morning and find it all never happened? We won't wake up and find we dreamed everything?"

"If only one of us does," Meg said, "and nobody else remembers any of it, then it's a dream. But if we all wake up remembering, then it really happened."

"Wait until tomorrow to find what tomorrow holds," Blajeny advised. "Good night, my children."

They did not ask him where he was going to spend the night—though Meg wondered—because it was the kind of presumptuous question one could not possibly ask Blajeny. They left him standing and watching after them, the folds of his robes chiseled like granite, his dark face catching and refracting the moonlight like fused glass.

They crossed the orchard and garden and entered the house, as usual, by the back way, through the pantry. The door to the lab was open, and the lights on. Mrs. Murry was bent over her microscope, and Dr. Colubra was curled up in an old red leather chair, reading. The lab was a long, narrow room with great slabs of stone for the floor. It had originally been used to keep milk and butter and other perishables, long before the days of refrigerators, and it was still difficult to heat in winter. The long work counter with the stone sink at one end was ideal for Mrs. Murry's lab equipment. In one corner were two comfortable chairs and a reading lamp, which softened the clinical glare of the lights over the counter. But Meg could not think of a time when she had seen her mother relaxing in one of those chairs; she inevitably perched on one of the lab stools.

She looked up from the strange convolutions of the microelectron microscope. "Charles! What are you doing out of bed?"

"I woke up," Charles Wallace said blandly. "I knew Meg and Calvin were outside, so I went to get them."

Mrs. Murry glanced sharply at her son, then greeted Calvin warmly.

Charles Wallace asked, "Is it okay if we make some cocoa?"

"It's very late for you to be up, Charles, and tomorrow's a school day."

"It'll help me get back to sleep."

Mrs. Murry seemed about to refuse, but Dr. Colubra closed her book, saying, "Why not, for once? Let Charles have a nap when he gets home in the afternoon. I'd like some cocoa myself. Let's make it out here while your mother goes on with her work. I'll do it."

"I'll get the milk and stuff from the kitchen," Meg said.

With Dr. Louise present they were not, she felt, free to talk to their mother about the events of the evening. The children were all fond of Dr. Louise, and trusted her completely as a physician, but they were not quite sure that she had their parents' capacity to accept the extraordinary. Almost sure, but not quite. Dr. Colubra had a good deal in common with their parents; she, too, had given up work which paid extremely well in both money and prestige, to come live in this small rural village. ('Too many of my colleagues have forgotten that they are supposed to practice the *art* of healing. If I don't have the gift of healing in my hands, then all my expensive training isn't worth very much.') She, too, had turned her back on the glitter of worldly success. Meg knew that her parents, despite the fact that they were consulted by the President of the United States, had given up much when they moved to the country in order to devote their lives to pure research. Their discoveries, many of them made in this stone laboratory, had made the Murrys more, rather than less, open to the strange, to the mysterious, to the unexplainable. Dr. Colubra's work was perforce more straightforward, and Meg was not sure how she would respond to talk of a strange dark Teacher, eight or nine feet tall, and even less sure how she would react to their description of a cherubim. She'd probably insist they were suffering from mass psychosis and that they all should see a psychiatrist at once.

—Or is it just that I'm afraid to talk about it, even to Mother? Meg wondered, as she took sugar, cocoa, milk, and a saucepan from the kitchen and returned to the pantry.

Dr. Colubra was saying, "That stuff about cosmic screams and rips in distant galaxies offends every bit of the rational part of me."

Mrs. Murry leaned against the counter. "You didn't believe in farandolae, either, until I proved them to you."

69

"You haven't proven them to me," Dr. Louise said. "Yet." She looked slightly ruffled, like a little grey bird. Her short, curly hair was grey; her eyes were grey above a small beak of a nose; she wore a grey flannel suit. "The main reason I think you may be right is that you go to that idiot machine—" she pointed at the micro-electron microscope—"the way my husband used to go to his violin. It was always like a lovers' meeting."

Mrs. Murry turned away from her 'idiot machine.' "I think I wish I'd never heard of farandolae, much less come to the conclusions—" She stopped abruptly, then said, "By the way, kids, I was rather surprised, just before you all barged into the lab, to have Mr. Jenkins call to suggest that we give Charles Wallace lessons in self-defense."

Mr. Jenkins? Meg wondered. Aloud she said, "But Mr. Jenkins never calls parents. Parents have to go to him." She almost asked, 'Are you *sure* it was Mr. Jenkins?' And stopped herself as she remembered that she had not told Blajeny about the horrible Mr. Jenkins-not-Mr. Jenkins who had turned into a bird of nothingness, the Mr. Jenkins Louise had resented so fiercely. She should have told Blajeny; she would tell him first thing in the morning.

Charles Wallace climbed up onto one of the lab stools and perched close to his mother. "What I really need are lessons in adaptation. I've been reading Darwin, but he hasn't helped me much."

"See what we mean?" Calvin asked Dr. Louise. "That's hardly what one expects from a six-year-old."

"He really does read Darwin," Meg assured the doctor.

70

"And I still haven't learned how to adapt," Charles Wallace added.

Dr. Louise was making a paste of cocoa, sugar, and a little hot water from one of Mrs. Murry's retorts. "This *is* just water, isn't it?" she asked.

"From our artesian well. The very best water."

Dr. Louise added milk, little by little. "You kids are too young to remember, and your mother is a good ten years younger than I am, but I'll never forget, a great many years ago, when the first astronauts went to the moon, and I sat up all night to watch them."

"I remember it all right," Mrs. Murry said. "I wasn't that young."

Dr. Louise stirred the cocoa which was heating over a Bunsen burner. "Do you remember those first steps on the moon, so tentative to begin with, on that strange, airless, alien terrain? And then, in a short time, Armstrong and Aldrin were striding about confidently, and the commentator remarked on this as an extraordinary example of man's remarkable ability to adapt."

"But all they had to adapt to was the moon's surface!" Meg objected. "It wasn't inhabited. I'll bet when our astronauts reach some place with inhabitants it won't be so easy. It's a lot simpler to adapt to low gravity, or no atmosphere, or even sandstorms, than it is to hostile inhabitants."

Fortinbras, who had an uncanine fondness for cocoa, came padding out to the lab, his nose twitching in anticipation. He stood on his hind legs and put his front paws on Charles Wallace's shoulders.

71

Dr. Colubra asked Meg, "Do you think the first-graders in the village school are hostile inhabitants, then?"

"Of course! Charles isn't like them, and so they're hostile towards him. People are always hostile to anybody who's different."

"Until they get used to him," the doctor said.

"They're not getting used to Charles."

Charles Wallace, fondling the big dog, said, "Don't forget to give Fort a saucer—he likes cocoa."

"You have the strangest pets," Dr. Louise said, but she poured a small dish of cocoa for Fortinbras. "I'll let it cool a bit before I put it on the floor. Meg, we need mugs."

"Okay." Meg hurried off to the kitchen, collected a stack of mugs, and returned to the laboratory.

Dr. Louise lined them up and poured the cocoa. "Speaking of pets, how's my namesake?"

Meg nearly spilled the cocoa she was handing to her mother. She looked closely at Dr. Louise, but though the question had seemed pointed, the little bird face showed nothing more than amused interest; as Charles Wallace said, Dr. Louise was very good at talking on one level and thinking on another.

Charles Wallace answered the question. "Louise the Larger is a magnificent snake. I wonder if she'd like some cocoa? Snakes like milk, don't they?"

Mrs. Murry said firmly, "You are not going back out tonight to find if the snake, magnificent though she be, likes cocoa. Save your experimental zeal for daylight. Louise is undoubtedly sound asleep."

72

Dr. Louise carefully poured out the last of the cocoa into her own mug. "Some snakes are very sociable at night. Many years ago when I was working in a hospital in the Philippines I had a boa constrictor for a pet; we had a problem with rats in the ward, and my boa constrictor did a thorough job of keeping the rodent population down. He also liked cream-of-mushroom soup, though I never tried him on cocoa, and he was a delightful companion in the evenings, affectionate and cuddly."

Meg did not think that she would enjoy cuddling with a snake, even Louise.

"He also had impeccable judgment about human nature. He was naturally a friendly creature, and if he showed me that he disliked or distrusted somebody, I took him seriously. We had a man brought to the men's ward who seemed to have nothing more seriously wrong with him than a slightly inflamed appendix, but my boa constrictor took a dislike to him the moment he was admitted. That night he tried to kill the man in the next bed—fortunately we got to him in time. But the snake knew. After that, I listened to his warnings immediately."

"Fortinbras has the same instinct about people," Mrs. Murry said. "Too bad we human beings have lost it."

Meg wanted to say, "So does Louise the Larger," but her mother or the doctor would have asked her on what experience she based such a remark; it would have sounded more likely coming from the twins.

Charles Wallace regarded Dr. Colubra, who had returned to the red leather chair and was sipping cocoa, her legs tucked under her like a child; as a matter of fact, she was considerably smaller than Meg. Charles said, "We take Louise very seriously, Dr. Louise. Very seriously."

Dr. Louise nodded. Her voice was light and high. "That was what I had in mind."

Calvin finished his cocoa. "Thank you very much. I'd better get on home now. See you in school tomorrow, Meg. Thanks again, Mrs. Murry and Dr. Colubra. Good night."

When he had gone, Mrs. Murry said, "All right, Charles. The twins have been in bed for an hour. Meg, it's time for you, too. Charles, I'll come check on you in a few minutes."

As they left the lab, Meg could see her mother turning back to the micro-electron microscope.

Meg undressed slowly, standing by her attic window, wondering if Dr. Louise's talk about snakes had been entirely casual chat over a cup of cocoa; perhaps it was only the strange events of the evening which caused her to look for meanings under the surface of what might well be unimportant conversation. She turned out the lights and looked out the window. She could see across the vegetable garden to the orchard, but the trees still held enough leaves so that she could not see into the north pasture.

Was there really a cherubim waiting at the star-watching rock, curled up into a great feathery ball, all those eyes closed in sleep?

Was he real?

What is real?

4 Proginoskes

Meg woke up before dawn, suddenly and completely, as though something had jerked her out of sleep. She listened: only the usual noises of the sleeping house. She turned on the light and looked at her clock; she had set the alarm for six, as usual. It was now five. She had another whole hour in which she could curl up under the covers, and luxuriate in warmth and comfort, and doze—

Then she remembered.

She tried to reassure herself that she was remembering a dream, although it was not the way that a dream is remembered. It must have been a dream, obviously it must have been a dream—

The only way to prove that it was nothing but a dream, without waking Charles Wallace and asking him, was to get dressed and go out to the star-watching rock and make sure that there was no cherubim there. And—if by some slim chance it had not been a dream, she had promised the cherubim that she would come to him before breakfast.

Had it not been for the horrible moments with Mr Jenkins screeching across the sky, she would not have wanted it to be a dream. She desperately wanted Blajeny to be real, to take care of everything. But the unreality of Mr. Jenkins, who had always been disagreeably predictable, was far more difficult for her to accept than the Teacher, or even a cherubim who looked like a drive of dragons.

She dressed hurriedly, putting on her kilt and a clean blouse. She tiptoed downstairs as quietly and carefully as she had the night before, through the kitchen and into the pantry, where she put on her heaviest jacket, and a multicolored knitted tam o'shanter, one of her mother's rare successful ventures into domesticity.

This time no wind blew, no doors slammed. She turned on the flashlight to guide her. It was a still, chill pre-dawn. The grass was white with spider-web tracings of dew and light frost. A thin vapor moved delicately across the lawn. The mountains were curtained by ground fog, although in the sky she could see stars. She ran across the garden, looking warily about her. But there was no Mr. Jenkins, of course there was no Mr. Jenkins. At the stone wall she looked carefully for Louise, but there was no sign of the big snake. She crossed the orchard, climbed the wall again —still no Louise, it was much too early and much too cold for snakes, anyhow—and ran across the north pasture, past the two glacial rocks, and to the star-watching rock.

There was nothing there except the mist whirling gently in the faint breeze.

So it had all been a dream.

Then the mist seemed to solidify, to become moving wings, eyes opening and shutting, tiny flickers of fire, small puffs of misty smoke . . .

"You're real," she said loudly. "You're not something I dreamed after all."

Proginoskes delicately stretched one huge wing skywards,

then folded it. "I have been told that human beings seldom dream about cherubim. Thank you for being prompt. It is in the nature of cherubim to dislike tardiness."

Meg sighed, in resignation, in fear, and, surprisingly, in relief. "Okay, Progo, I guess you're not a figment of my imagination. What do we do now? I've got just about an hour before breakfast."

"Are you hungry?"

"No, I'm much too excited to be hungry, but if I don't turn up on time, it won't go down very well if I explain that I was late because I was talking with a cherubim. My mother doesn't like tardiness, either."

Proginoskes said, "Much can be accomplished in an hour. We have to find out what our first ordeal is."

"Don't you know?"

"Why would I know?"

"You're a cherubim."

"Even a cherubim has limits. When three ordeals are planned, then nobody knows ahead of time what they are; even the Teacher may not know."

"Then what do we do? How do we find out?"

Proginoskes waved several wings slowly back and forth in thought, which would have felt very pleasant on a hot day, but which, on a cold morning, made Meg turn up the collar of her jacket. The cherubim did not notice; he continued waving and thinking Then she could feel his words moving slowly, tentatively, within her mind. "If you've been assigned to me, I suppose you must be some kind of a Namer, too, even if a primitive one."

"A what?"

77

"A Namer. For instance, the last time I was with a Teacher—or at school, as you call it—my assignment was to memorize the names of the stars."

"Which stars?"

"All of them."

"You mean *all* the stars, in *all* the galaxies?"

"Yes. If he calls for one of them, someone has to know which one he means. Anyhow, they like it; there aren't many who know them all by name, and if your name isn't known, then it's a very lonely feeling."

"Am I supposed to learn the names of all the stars, too?" It was an appalling thought.

"Good galaxy, no!"

"Then what *am* I supposed to do?"

Proginoskes waved several wings, which, Meg was learning, was more or less his way of expressing "I haven't the faintest idea."

"Well, then, if I'm a Namer, what does that mean? What does a Namer do?"

The wings drew together, the eyes closed, singly, and in groups, until all were shut. Small puffs of mist-like smoke rose, swirled about him. "When I was memorizing the names of the stars, part of the purpose was to help them each to be more particularly the particular star each one was supposed to be. That's basically a Namer's job. Maybe you're supposed to make earthlings feel more human."

"What's that supposed to mean?" She sat down on the rock beside him; she was somehow no longer afraid of his wildness, his size, his spurts of fire.

He asked, "How do I make you feel?"

She hesitated, not wanting to be rude, forgetting that the cherubim, far more than Charles Wallace, did not need her outward words to know what was being said within. But she answered truthfully, "Confused."

Several puffs of smoke went up. "Well, we don't know each other very well yet. Who makes you least confused?"

"Calvin." There was no hesitation here. "When I'm with Calvin, I don't mind being me."

"You mean he makes you *more* you, don't you?"

"I guess you could put it that way."

"Who makes you feel the least you?"

"Mr. Jenkins."

Proginoskes probed sharply, "Why are you suddenly upset and frightened?"

"He's the principal of the grade school in the village this year. But he was in my school last year, and I was always getting sent to his office. He never understands anything, and everything I do is automatically wrong. Charles Wallace would probably be better off if he weren't my brother. That's enough to finish him with Mr. Jenkins."

"Is that all?"

"What do you mean?"

"When you say *Mr. Jenkins,* I feel such a cold wave of terror wash over you that I feel chilly myself."

"Progo—something happened last night—before we met you and Blajeny—when I was all alone in the garden—" Her voice tailed off.

"*What* happened, earthling? Tell me. I have a feeling this may be important."

Why should it be difficult to tell Proginoskes? The cherubim himself was just as unbelievable. But the cherubim was himself, was Proginoskes, while Mr. Jenkins had not been Mr. Jenkins.

As she tried to explain to Proginoskes she could sense him pulling away, and suddenly he flung all his wings about himself in a frantic reflex of self-preservation. Then two eyes looked out at her under one wing. "Echthroi." It was an ugly word. As Proginoskes uttered it the morning seemed colder.

"What did you say?" Meg asked.

"Your Mr. Jenkins—the real one—could he do anything like the one you just told me about? Could he fly into a nothingness in the sky? This is not a thing that human beings can do, is it?"

"No."

"You say he was like a dark bird, but a bird that was nothingness, and that he tore the sky?"

"Well—that's how I remember it. It was all quick and unexpected and I was terrified and I couldn't really believe that it had happened."

"It sounds like the Echthroi." He covered his eyes again.

"The what?"

Slowly, as though with a great effort, he uncovered several eyes. "The Echthroi. Oh, earthling, if you do not know Echthroi—"

"I don't want to. Not if they're like what I saw last night."

Proginoskes agitated his wings. "I think we must go see this Mr. Jenkins, the one you say is at your little brother's school."

"Why?"

Proginoskes withdrew into all his wings again. Meg could feel him thinking grumpily, —They told me it was going to be difficult . . . Why couldn't they have sent me off some place *quiet* to recite the stars again? . . . Or I'm even willing to memorize farandolae . . . I've never been to Earth before, I'm too young, I'm scared of the shadowed planets, what kind of a star has this planet got, anyhow?

Then he emerged, slowly, one pair of eyes at a time. "Megling, I think you have seen an Echthros. If we are dealing with Echthroi, then—I just know with every feather on my wings (and you might try counting my feathers, sometime) that we have to go see this Mr. Jenkins. It must be part of the trial."

"Mr. Jenkins? Part of our first test? But that's—it doesn't make sense."

"It does to me."

"Progo," she objected, "it's impossible. I can slip off my school bus and then walk to the grade school the way I did when I went to talk to Mr. Jenkins about Charles Wallace— and a fat lot of good *that* did—"

"If you have seen an Echthros, everything is different," Proginoskes said.

"Okay, I can get to the grade school all right, but I can't possibly take you with me. You're so big you wouldn't even fit into the school bus. Anyhow, you'd terrify everybody." At the thought she smiled, but Proginoskes was not in a laughing mood.

"Not everybody is able to see me," he told her. "I'm real, and most earthlings can bear very little reality. But if it will relieve your mind, I'll dematerialize." He waved a few wings gracefully. "It's really more comfortable for me not to be burdened with matter, but I thought it would be easier for you if you could converse with someone you could see."

The cherubim was there in front of her, covering most of the star-watching rock, and then he was not there. She thought she saw a faint shimmer in the air, but it might have been the approach of dawn. She could feel him, however, moving within her mind. "Are you feeling extremely brave, Megling?"

"No." A faint light defined the eastern horizon. The stars were dim, almost extinguished.

"I think we're going to have to be brave, earth child, but it will be easier because we're together. I wonder if the Teacher knows."

"Knows what?"

"That you've seen an Echthros."

"Progo, I don't understand. What is an Echthros?"

Abruptly, Proginoskes materialized, raised several wings, and gathered her in. "Come, littleling. I'll take you some place yesterday and show you."

"How can you take me yesterday?"

"I can't possibly take you today, silly. It's time for you to go in to breakfast and your mother dislikes tardiness. And who knows what we may have to do or where we may have to go before tomorrow? Come." He drew her further in to him.

She found herself looking directly into one of his eyes, a great, amber cat's eye, the dark mandala of the pupil, opening, compelling, beckoning.

82

She was drawn towards the oval, was pulled into it, was through it.

Into the ultimate night on the other side.

Then she felt a great, flaming wind, and knew that somehow she herself was part of that wind.

Then she felt a great shove, and she was standing on a bare stone mountain top, and Proginoskes was blinking and winking at her. She thought she saw the oval, mandala-eye through which she had come, but she was not sure.

The cherubim raised a great wing to sketch the slow curve of sky above them. The warm rose and lavender of sunset faded, dimmed, was extinguished. The sky was drenched with green at the horizon, muting upwards into a deep, purply blue through which stars began to appear in totally unfamiliar constellations.

Meg asked, "Where are we?"

"Never mind where. Watch."

She stood beside him, looking at the brilliance of the stars. Then came a sound, a sound which was above sound, beyond sound, a violent, silent, electrical report, which made her press her hands in pain against her ears. Across the sky, where the stars were clustered as thickly as in the Milky Way, a crack shivered, slivered, became a line of nothingness.

If this kind of thing was happening in the universe, no matter how far away from earth and the Milky Way, Meg did not wonder that her father had been summoned to Washington and Brookhaven.

"Progo, what is it? What happened?"

"The Echthroi have Xed."

"What?"

"Annihilated. Negated. Extinguished. Xed."

Meg stared in horrible fascination at the rent in the sky. This was the most terrible thing she had ever seen, more horrifying than the Mr. Jenkins-Echthros the night before. She pressed close to the cherubim, surrounding herself with wings and eyes and puffs of smoke, but she could still see the rip in the sky.

She could not bear it.

She closed her eyes to shut it out. She tried to think of the most comfortable thing possible, the safest, most reasonable, ordinary thing. What, then? The dinner table at home: winter: the red curtains drawn across the windows, and a quiet snow falling softly outdoors; an applewood fire in the fireplace and Fortinbras snoring happily on the hearth; a tape playing Holst's *The Planets*—no, maybe that wasn't too comforting; in her mind's ear she shifted to a ghastly recording of the school band, with Sandy and Dennys playing somewhere in the cacophony.

Dinner was over, and she was clearing the table and starting the dishes and only half listening to the conversation of her parents, who were lingering over their coffee.

It was almost as tangible as though she were actually there, and she thought she felt Proginoskes pushing at her mind, helping her remember.

Had she really listened that attentively to her parents while she stood running hot water over the plates? Their voices were as clear as though she were actually in the room.

Her father must have mentioned the terrible thing which Proginoskes had just shown her, the terrible thing which was terrible precisely because it was not a thing, because it was nothing. She could hear, too clearly, her father's voice, calm and rational, speaking to her mother. "It isn't just in distant galaxies that strange, unreasonable things are happening. Unreason has crept up on us so insidiously that we've hardly been aware of it. But think of the things going on in our own country which you wouldn't have believed possible only a few years ago."

Mrs. Murry swirled the dregs of her coffee. "I don't think I believe all of them now, although I know they're happening." She looked up to see that the twins and Charles Wallace were out of the room, that Meg was splashing water in the sink as she scoured a pot. "Ten years ago we didn't even have a key to this house. Now we lock up when we go out. The irrational violence is even worse in the cities."

Mr. Murry absent-mindedly began working out an equation on the tablecloth. For once Mrs. Murry did not even seem to notice. He said, "They've never known a time when people drank rain water because it was pure, or could eat snow, or swim in any river or brook. The last time I drove home from Washington the traffic was so bad I could have made better time with a horse. There were huge signs proclaiming SPEED LIMIT 65 MPH, and we were crawling along at 20."

"And the children and I kept dinner hot for you for three hours, and finally ate, pretending we weren't worried that you might have been in an accident," Mrs. Murry said

85

bitterly. "Here we are, at the height of civilization in a well-run state in a great democracy. And four ten-year-olds were picked up last week for pushing hard drugs in the school where our six-year-old is regularly given black eyes and a bloody nose." She suddenly noticed the equation growing on the tablecloth. "What are you doing?"

"I have a hunch that there's some connection between your discoveries about the effects of farandolae on mitochondria, and that unexplained phenomenon out in space." His pencil added a fraction, some Greek characters, and squared them.

Mrs. Murry said in a low voice, "My discoveries are not very pleasant."

"I know."

"I isolated farandolae because something beyond increasing air pollution has to account for the accelerating number of deaths from respiratory failure, and this so-called flu epidemic. It was the micro-sonarscope which gave me the first clue—" She stopped abruptly, looked at her husband. "It's the same sound, isn't it? The strange 'cry' of the ailing mitochondria, and the 'cry' picked up in those distant galaxies by the new paraboloidoscope—there's a horrid similarity between them. I don't like it. I don't like the fact that we don't even see what's going on in our own back yard. L.A. is trying as honorably as a president can try in a world which has become so blunted by dishonor and violence that people casually take it for granted. We have to see a great, dramatic fissure in the sky before we begin to take danger seriously. And I have to be deathly worried about our

86

youngest child before I regard farandolae except in a cool and academic manner."

Meg had turned from the kitchen sink at the pain in her mother's voice, and had seen her father reach across the table for her mother's hand. "My dear, this is not like you. With my intellect I see cause for nothing but pessimism and even despair. But I can't settle for what my intellect tells me. That's not all of it."

"What else is there?" Mrs. Murry's voice was low and anguished.

"There are still stars which move in ordered and beautiful rhythm. There are still people in this world who keep promises. Even little ones, like your cooking stew over your Bunsen burner. You may be in the middle of an experiment, but you still remember to feed your family. That's enough to keep my heart optimistic, no matter how pessimistic my mind. And you and I have good enough minds to know how very limited and finite they really are. The naked intellect is an extraordinarily inaccurate instrument."

Proginoskes said, "He's a wise man, your father."

"Could you hear me remembering?"

"I was remembering with you. Most of that conversation you didn't hear with your conscious mind, you know."

"I have a very good memory—" Meg started. Then she stopped herself. "Okay. I know I couldn't have remembered all that by myself. I suppose I just sort of took in the sound waves, didn't I? But how did you get it all from me?"

Proginoskes looked at her with two, ringed owl-like eyes. "You're beginning to learn how to kythe."

"To what?"

"Kythe. It's how cherubim talk. It's talking without words, just the same way that I can be myself and not be enfleshed."

"But I have to be enfleshed, and I need words."

"I know, Meg," he replied gently, "and I will keep things worded for you. But it will help if you will remember that cherubim kythe without words among each other. For a human creature you show a distinct talent for kything."

She blushed slightly at the compliment; she had a feeling that paying compliments is a habit not often indulged in by cherubim. "Progo, I wish I'd been able to see the equation Father was doodling on the tablecloth. If I'd seen it, then it might be somewhere in my mind for you to pull out."

"Think," Proginoskes said. "I'll help."

"Mother put the tablecloth in the wash."

"But you remember there were some Greek letters."

"Yes . . ."

"Let me try to find them with you."

She closed her eyes.

"That's right. Relax, now. Maybe this is the way for us to kythe. —Don't you try to think. Just let me move about."

Out of the corner of her mind's eye she seemed to see three Greek characters among the numbers in the loosely strung equation her father was scribbling on the cloth. She thought them at Proginoskes.

"$\epsilon \chi \theta$. Epsilon, chi, and theta. That's Echth," the cherubim told her.

"Echthroi—but how could Father—"

"Think of the conversation we just recalled, Meg. Your parents are very aware of the evil in the world."

"All right. Yes. I know. Okay." Meg sounded cross. "Until Charles started school I hoped maybe we could ignore it. Like ostriches or something."

The cherubim withdrew its wings from her entirely, leaving her exposed and cold on the strange hilltop. "Open your eyes and look where the sky is torn."

"I'd rather not."

"Go on. I've got all my eyes open, and you only have to open two."

Meg opened her eyes. The rent in the sky was still there. She wondered what this distant phenomenon could have to do with Charles Wallace's pallor, with mitochondritis, or whatever it was. "How—oh, Progo, how did the Echthroi do that?"

Like Charles Wallace, he picked up her particular anxiety. "It has to do with un-Naming. If we are Namers, the Echthroi are un-Namers, non-Namers."

"Progo, what does that have to do with Mr. Jenkins?"

She felt a wave of apprehension roll through her. "Littleling, I think that is what we must find out. I think that it is part of our first ordeal. Let us go." He drew her back into himself again; again she was confronted with the single eye, was pulled through the opening, oval pupil. Then the pupil snapped shut, and they were together on the starwatching rock with dawn slowly lightening the east.

Progo spread his wings wide, and she moved out. "What do we do now?" he said.

The cherubim was asking *her?* "I am only a human being, not quite full-grown," she replied. "How would I know?"

"Megling, I've never been on your planet before. This is your home. Charles Wallace is your brother. You are the one who knows Mr. Jenkins. You must tell me what we are to do now."

Meg stamped, loudly and angrily, against the hard, cold surface of the rock. "This is too much responsibility! I'm still only a child! I didn't ask for any of this!"

"Are you refusing to take the test?" Proginoskes pulled away from her.

"But I didn't ask for it! I didn't ask for Blajeny, or you, or any of it!"

"Didn't you? I thought you were worried about Charles Wallace."

"I am! I'm worried about everything!"

"Meg." Proginoskes was somber and stern. "Are you going to enter into the ordeal? I must know. Now."

Meg stamped again. "Of course I'm going to. You know I have to. Charles Wallace is in danger. I'll do anything to help him, even if it seems silly."

"Then what do we do now?"

She shoved at her glasses as though that would help her think. "I'd better go home now and have breakfast. Then I'll get on my school bus—it stops at the bottom of the hill and maybe you'd better wait for me there. Fortinbras might bark at you; I'm sure he'd know you were in the house even if you dematerialize, or whatever you call it."

"Whatever you think best," Proginoskes said meekly.

"I'll be down at the foot of the road at seven o'clock. The high-school bus covers so much distance and makes so many stops it takes an hour and a half, and I get on at one of the first stops."

She felt an acquiescing response from the cherubim, and then he disappeared; she could not see even a shimmer, or feel a flicker of him in her mind. She headed back to the house. She kept the flashlight on, not for the known turnings of the path, but for whatever new, unknown surprises might be waiting for her.

When Meg got to the stone wall Louise the Larger was there. Waiting. Neither greeting nor attacking. Waiting. Meg approached her cautiously. Louise watched her through eyes which shone in the flashlight like the water of a very deep well.

"May I go by, please, Louise?" Meg asked timidly.

Louise uncoiled, waving slightly in greeting, still looking intently at Meg. Then she bowed her head, and slithered off into the rocks. Meg felt that Louise had been waiting for her to give her a warning for whatever lay ahead, and to wish her well. It was strangely comforting to know that Louise's well-wishing was going with her.

There was sausage as well as hot porridge for breakfast. Meg felt that she ought to eat heartily, because who knew what lay ahead? But she could manage only a few mouthfuls.

"Are you all right, Meg?" her mother asked.

"Fine. Thanks."

"You look a little pale. Sure you aren't coming down with something?"

—She's worried about all of us with this mitochondritis stuff. "Just the normal throes of adolescence," she smiled at her mother.

Sandy said, "If you don't want your sausage, I'll eat it."

Dennys said, "Half for me, okay?"

Charles Wallace slowly and deliberately ate a full bowl of porridge, but gave the twins his sausage.

"Well, then"—Meg washed her dishes and put them in the rack—"I'm off."

"Wait for us," Sandy said.

She did not want to wait for the twins, to listen to their chatter on the walk down to the bus. On the other hand, it would keep her from thinking about what lay ahead. She had thought of Mr. Jenkins for as far back as she could remember with distaste, annoyance, and occasionally outrage, but never before with fear.

When she left the house she had a horrid, premonitory feeling that it would be a long time before she returned. Again she wished that Fortinbras were walking to the bus with them, as he often did, and then returning to make the walk again with Charles Wallace. But this morning he showed no inclination to leave the warmth of the kitchen.

"What do you suppose will happen today?" Sandy asked as they started down the hill in the chill of early morning.

Dennys shrugged. "Nothing. As usual. Race you to the foot of the hill."

5 The First Test

Meg and the cherubim reached the deserted schoolyard in safety.

"We've got a while to wait," Meg told him, "and it's okay for you, you're invisible. But I've got to find a place to hide." She could not see Proginoskes, but she talked at the faint shimmer in the air where she knew he was.

"You're too late," the cherubim said, and Meg swung around to see Mr. Jenkins coming across the schoolyard from the faculty parking lot.

Mr. Jenkins. The ordinary, everyday, usual Mr. Jenkins. There was no snake hissing and clacking at him, and he himself did nothing but continue his way across the school-yard. He looked just as he always looked. He wore his usual dark business suit, and no matter how often it was brushed there was always a small snowfall of dandruff on his shoulders. His salt-and-pepper hair was cut short, and his eyes were muddy behind his bifocals. He was neither short nor tall, fat nor thin, and whenever Meg saw him her feet seemed to grow larger and she couldn't find a resting place for her hands.

"All right, Margaret, what is this? What are you doing here?" He had every right to sound annoyed.

She had nothing to reply. She felt Proginoskes close to

her, felt his mind within hers, but he had nothing to suggest.

"My dear child," Mr. Jenkins said, and his voice was unwontedly compassionate. "If you have come again about your little brother, I can now tell you that we are reviewing his case. It is not my policy of education to have one child intimidated by his peers. But our initial testing shows that Charles Wallace's talents are so unusual that unusual measures must be taken. I've had several consultations with the State Board, and we are considering getting a special tutor for him."

Meg looked warily at the principal. This sounded too good to be true.

And Louise had been trying to warn her of something. Of what?

The cherubim, too, was uneasy. She felt him moving lightly in her mind, feeling her response to this unexpectedly reasonable Mr. Jenkins.

"That is nonsense," Mr. Jenkins said to Mr. Jenkins. "We cannot make an exception for any one child. Charles Wallace Murry must learn to manage."

A second Mr. Jenkins was standing beside Mr. Jenkins. It was impossible. It was just as impossible as—

But there *were* two identical, dour Mr. Jenkinses standing in front of her.

Proginoskes shimmered, but did not materialize. Meg backed into the shimmer; she felt that the cherubim was opening an invisible wing and pulling her close to him. She could feel his tremendous, wild heartbeat, a frightened heartbeat, thundering in her ears.

"We're Namers," she heard through the racing of the heart. "We're Namers. What is their Name?"

"Mr. Jenkins."

"No, no. This is the test, Meg, it must be. One of those Mr. Jenkinses is an Echthros. We have to know which is the *real* Mr. Jenkins."

Meg looked at the two men who stood glaring at each other. "Progo, you can feel into me. Can't you feel into them? Can't you kythe?"

"Not when I don't know who they are. You're the one who knows the prototype."

"The what?"

"The real one. The only Mr. Jenkins who is Mr. Jenkins. Look—"

Suddenly beside the two Mr. Jenkinses stood a third Mr. Jenkins. He raised one hand in greeting, not to Meg, but to the other two men as he drew level with them. "Leave the poor girl alone for a few minutes," Mr. Jenkins Three said.

The three men wheeled, stiffly, like marionettes, and walked across the schoolyard and into the building.

"We must think. We must think." Proginoskes's kythe almost became opaque for a second, and Meg felt that he was restraining himself from spouting fire.

Meg said, "Progo, if you really are a cherubim—"

There was a great and surging invisible wave of indignation all around her.

She hit the clenched fist of one hand against the palm of the other. "Wait. You told me to think, and I'm thinking."

"You don't have to think out loud. You don't have to talk to think, after all. You're deafening me. Try to kythe with me, Meg."

"I still don't understand kything. Is it like mental telepathy?"

Proginoskes hesitated. "You might say that mental telepathy is the very beginning of learning to kythe. But the cherubic language is entirely kything—with you, with stars, with galaxies, with the salt in the ocean, the leaves of the trees."

"But I'm not a cherubim. How do I do it?"

"Meg, your brain stores all the sensory impressions it receives, but your conscious mind doesn't have a key to the storehouse. All I want you to do is to open yourself up to me so that I can open the door to your mind's storehouse."

"All right. I'll try." To open herself entirely to the cherubim, to make herself completely vulnerable, was not going to be easy. But she trusted Proginoskes implicitly. "Listen," she said, "cherubim have come to my planet before."

"I know that. Where do you think I got my information?"

"What do you know about us?"

"I have heard that your host planet is shadowed, that it is troubled."

"It's beautiful," Meg said defensively.

She felt a rippling of his wings. "In the middle of your cities?"

"Well—no—but I don't live in a city."

"And is your planet peaceful?"

"Well, no—it isn't very peaceful."

"I had the idea," Proginoskes moved reluctantly within her mind, "that there are wars on your planet. People fighting and killing each other."

"Yes, that's so, but—"

"And children go hungry."

"Yes."

"And people don't understand each other."

"Not always."

"And there's—there's hate?"

"Yes."

She felt Proginoskes pulling away. "All I want to do," he was murmuring to himself, "is go some place quiet and recite the names of the stars . . ."

"Progo! You said we were Namers. I still don't *know:* what *is* a Namer?"

"I've *told* you. A Namer has to know who people are, and who they are meant to be. I don't know why I should have been shocked at finding Echthroi on your planet."

"Why are they here?"

"Echthroi are always about when there's war. They start all war."

"Progo, I saw all that awfulness you took me to see, that tearing of the sky, and all, but you still haven't told me exactly what Echthroi are."

Proginoskes probed into her mind, searching for words she could understand. "I think your mythology would call them fallen angels. War and hate are their business, and

97

one of their chief weapons is un-Naming—making people not know who they are. If someone knows who he is, really knows, then he doesn't need to hate. That's why we still need Namers, because there are places throughout the universe like your planet Earth. When everyone is really and truly Named, then the Echthroi will be vanquished."

"But what—"

"Oh, earthling, earthling, why do you think Blajeny called for you? There is war in heaven, and we need all the help we can get. The Echthroi are spreading through the universe. Every time a star goes out another Echthros has won a battle. A star or a child or a farandola—size doesn't matter, Meg. The Echthroi are after Charles Wallace and the balance of the entire universe can be altered by the outcome."

"But Progo, what does this have to do with our test—and with three Mr. Jenkinses—it's insane."

Proginoskes responded coldly and quietly. "Precisely."

Into the cold and quiet came the sound of the school buses arriving, doors opening, children rushing out and into the school building.

Charles Wallace was one of those children.

Proginoskes moved quietly in her mind through the roar. "Don't misunderstand me, Meg. It is the ways of the Echthroi which are insane. The ways of the Teachers are often strange, but they are never haphazard. I know that Mr. Jenkins has to have something to do with it, something important, or we wouldn't be here."

Meg said, unhappily, "If I hate Mr. Jenkins whenever I think of him, am I Naming him?"

98

Proginoskes shifted his wings. "You're Xing him, just like the Echthroi."

"Progo!"

"Meg, when people don't know who they are, they are open either to being Xed, or Named."

"And you think I'm supposed to Name Mr. Jenkins?" It was a ridiculous idea; no matter how many Mr. Jenkinses there were, he was Mr. Jenkins. That's all.

But Proginoskes was most definite. "Yes."

Meg cried rebelliously, "Well, I think it's a silly kind of test."

"What you think is not the point. What you do is what's going to count."

"How can it possibly help Charles?"

"I don't know. We don't have to know everything at once. We just do one thing at a time, as it is given us to do."

"But how do I do it? How do I Name Mr. Jenkins when all I think of when I see him is how awful he is?"

Proginoskes sighed and flung several wings heavenwards so violently that he lifted several feet, materialized, and came down with a thud. "There's a word—but if I say it you'll just misunderstand."

"You have to say it."

"It's a four-letter word. Aren't four-letter words considered the bad ones on your planet?"

"Come on. I've seen all the four-letter words on the walls of the washroom at school."

Proginoskes let out a small puff. "Luff."

"What?"

"Love. That's what makes persons know who they are.

You're full of love, Meg, but you don't know how to stay within it when it's not easy."

"What do you mean?"

"Oh—you love your family. That's easy. Sometimes when you feel awful about somebody, you get back into rightness by thinking about—well, you seem to be telling me that you got back into love once by thinking about Charles Wallace."

"Yes—"

"But this time it can't be easy. You have to go on to the next step."

"If you mean you think I have to love Mr. Jenkins, you've got another think coming," Meg snapped.

Proginoskes gave a mighty sigh. "If we pass the test, you'll go on and be taught—oh, some of the things I was taught my first billennium with the Teachers. I had to pass a galaxy of tests before I could qualify as a Star Namer. But you're a human being, and it's all quite different with you. I keep forgetting that. Am I lovable? To you?"

All about Meg, eyes opened and shut; wings shifted; a small flame burned her hand and was rapidly withdrawn. She coughed and then sucked the burned place on her hand. But all she wanted was to put her arms around Proginoskes as she would around Charles Wallace. "Very lovable," she said.

"But you don't love me the way you love that skinny Calvin?"

"That's different."

"I thought so. That's the confusing kind. Not the kind you have to have in order to Name Mr. Jenkins."

"I hate Mr. Jenkins."

"Meg, it's the test. You have to Name the real Mr. Jenkins, and I have to help you. If you fail, I fail too."

"Then what would happen?"

"It's your first time with a Teacher. And it would be your last."

"And you?"

"When one has been with the Teachers as often as I have, one is given a choice. I could throw in my lot with the Echthroi—"

"What!"

"Quite a few of those who fail do."

"But the Echthroi are—"

"You know what they are. Sky tearers. Light snuffers. Planet darkeners. The dragons. The worms. Those who hate."

"Progo, you couldn't."

"I hope I couldn't. But others have. It's not an easy choice."

"If you don't go to the Echthroi—"

All Proginoskes's eyes were shielded by his wings. "I am a Namer. The Echthroi would un-Name. If I do not go with them, then I must X myself."

"What!?"

"I'll ask you a riddle. What do you have the more of, the more of it you give away?"

"Oh, love, I suppose."

"So, if I care more about Naming than anything else, then maybe I have to give myself away, if it's the only way to show my love. All the way away. To X myself."

"If you do it—X yourself—does it last forever?" Meg asked apprehensively.

"Nobody knows. Nobody will know till the end of time."

"Do I have that choice, too, if—if we fail?" She turned away from the school building, towards the early-morning shouts and whistles, and pressed her face against the soft feathers of one great pinion.

"It is not an option given to mortals, earthling."

"All that happens to me is that I go home?"

"If you can call it *all*. There would be rejoicing in hell. But perhaps you don't believe in hell?"

Meg pushed this aside. "But if we fail, then you—"

"I must choose. It's better to X myself than to be Xed by the Echthroi."

"What you took me to see—it was what Mother talked about at the dinner table, what Father's gone to Brookhaven about—it doesn't seem to have much to do with Mr. Jenkins. It's all so cosmic, so big—"

"It isn't size that matters, Meg. Right now it's Charles Wallace. The Echthroi would annihilate Charles Wallace."

"A little boy!"

"You've said yourself that he's a special little boy."

"He is, oh, he is." She gave a startled jump as the first bell went off inside the school building, strident, demanding. "Progo, I don't understand any of it, but if you think Naming Mr. Jenkins is going to help Charles Wallace, I'll do my best. You *will* help me?"

"I'll try." But Proginoskes did not sound confident.

From all around them came the usual schoolday din.

102

Then the door to the cafeteria/gym opened, and a Mr. Jenkins came out. Which Mr. Jenkins? There was no telling them apart. Meg looked to the cherubim, but he had dematerialized again, leaving only a shimmer to show where he was.

Mr. Jenkins came to her. She checked his shoulders. There was the dandruff. She went closer: smelled: yes, he had the Mr. Jenkins smell of old hair cream and what she always thought of as rancid deodorant. But all three of the Mr. Jenkinses could manage that much, she was sure. It was not going to be that easy.

He looked at her coldly in the usual way, down one side of his slightly crooked nose. "I assume that you are as confused by all this as I am, Margaret. Why two strange men should wish to impersonate me I have no idea. It is most inconvenient, just at the beginning of school, when I am already overworked. I am told that it has something to do with you as well as your unfortunate little brother. I had hoped that this year you, at least, would not be one of my problems. It seems to me I have had to spend more time with you than with any other student in school. It is certainly my misfortune. And now not only do I have to cope with your little brother, who is equally difficult, but here you are again."

This was Mr. Jenkins. He had played upon the theme of this speech with infinite variations almost every time she was sent to his office.

"For some reason obscure to me, you are supposed to choose between the impostors and me. It is certainly in my

103

interests to have you pass this absurd test. Then perhaps I can keep you out of my school."

"And then," said Mr. Jenkins Two, appearing beside Mr. Jenkins One, "I will have time to concentrate on present problems instead of those which ought to be past. Now, Meg, if you will just for once in your life do it my way, not yours . . . I understand you're basically quite bright in mathematics. If you would simply stop approaching each problem in your life as though you were Einstein and had to solve the problems of the universe, and would deign to follow one or two basic rules, you—and I—would have a great deal less trouble."

This, too, was authentic Jenkins.

The shimmer of the cherubim wavered uneasily.

"Meg," Mr. Jenkins Two said, "I urge you to resolve this nonsense and tell the impostors that I am Mr. Jenkins. This whole farce is wasting a great deal of time. I am Mr. Jenkins, as you have cause to know."

She felt Proginoskes probing wildly. "Meg, when have you been most *you,* the very most *you?*"

She closed her eyes. She remembered the first afternoon Calvin had come to the Murrys'. Calvin was an honor student, but he was far better with words than with numbers, and Meg had helped him with a trigonometry problem. Since trig was not taught in Meg's grade, her easy competence was one of her first surprises for Calvin. But at the time she had not thought of surprising him. She had concentrated wholly on Calvin, on what he was doing, and she had felt wholly alive and herself.

"How is that going to help?" she asked the cherubim.

"Think. You didn't know Calvin very well then, did you?"

"No."

"But you loved him, didn't you?"

"Then? I wasn't thinking about love. I was just thinking about trig."

"Well, then," Proginoskes said, as though that explained the entire nature of love.

"But I can't think about trig with Mr. Jenkins. And I can't love him."

"You love me."

"But, Progo, you're so awful you're lovable."

"So is he. And you have to Name him."

A third Mr. Jenkins joined the other two. "Meg. Stop panicking and listen to me."

The three men stood side by side, identical, grey, dour, unperceptive, overworked: unlovable.

"Meg," Mr. Jenkins Two said, "if you will Name me, and quickly, I will see to it that Charles Wallace gets into competent medical hands immediately."

"It's hardly that easy," Mr. Jenkins Three said. "After all, her parents—"

"—do not know how to handle the situation, nor do they understand how serious it is," Mr. Jenkins Two snapped.

Mr. Jenkins Three waved this aside. "Meg, does it not seem extraordinary to you that you should be confronted with three of me?"

There seemed to be no answer to this question.

Mr. Jenkins One shrugged in annoyance.

Mr. Jenkins Two said, "It is imperative that we stick to essentials at this point. Our number is peripheral." The real Mr. Jenkins was very fond of discarding peripherals and sticking to essentials.

Mr. Jenkins Three said, "That there is only one of me, and that I am he, is the main point."

Mr. Jenkins Two snorted. "Except for the small but important fact that I am he. This trial that has been brought on us is an extraordinary one. None of us—that is, you and I, Margaret—will ever be the same again. Being confronted with these two mirror visions of myself has made me see myself differently. None of us likes to see himself as he must appear to others. I understand your point of view much better than I did before. You were quite right to come to me about your little brother. He is indeed special, and I have come to the conclusion that I have made a mistake in not realizing this, and treating him accordingly."

"Don't trust him," Mr. Jenkins Three said.

Mr. Jenkins Two swept on. "I believe that you and I had a—shall we call it a run-in?—over the imports and exports of Nicaragua, which you were supposed to learn for one of your social-studies classes. You were quite right when you insisted that it was unnecessary for you to learn the imports and exports of Nicaragua. I shall try not to make the same kind of mistake with Charles Wallace. If Charles Wallace's interests are different from those of our usual first-grader, we will try to understand that he has been taught by an eminent physicist father. I am sorry for all the needless pain you have been caused. And I can assure you that if you Name me, Charles Wallace will find school a pleasanter place, and I have no doubt his health will improve."

Meg looked warily at Mr. Jenkins Two. This was, indeed, a changed Mr. Jenkins, and she did not trust the change. On the other hand, she remembered vividly the battle they had had over the imports and exports of Nicaragua.

Mr. Jenkins Three murmured, "Methinks the gentleman doth protest too much."

Mr. Jenkins Two sputtered, "What's that?" Mr. Jenkins One looked blank.

Mr. Jenkins Three cried triumphantly, "I could have told you he would not recognize Shakespeare. He is an impostor."

Meg had her doubts whether or not the real Mr. Jenkins would recognize Shakespeare.

Mr. Jenkins Two said, "Shakespeare is peripheral. If I have often been irritable in the past it is because I have been worried. Despite your unkind opinion of me, I do not like seeing any of my children unhappy." He sniffed.

Mr. Jenkins One looked down his nose. "If I had the co-operation of the School Board and the P.T.A. it might untie my hands so that I could accomplish something."

Meg looked at the three men in their identical business suits. "It's like a game on television."

"It is not a game," Mr. Jenkins Three said sharply. "The stakes are much too high."

Meg asked, "What happens to you—all of you—if I Name the wrong one?"

For a moment all the atoms of air in the schoolyard

seemed to shiver; it was as though a lightning bolt of nothingness had flashed across the schoolyard, ripping the fabric of the atmosphere, then closed together again. Although nothing had been visible, Meg thought of a dark and terrible vulture slashing across the sky.

Mr. Jenkins One said, "I do not believe in the supernatural. But this entire situation is abnormal." His rabbity nose wriggled in pink distaste.

Then all three men swung around as the side door to the school opened, and Charles Wallace, Louise the Larger twined around his arm and shoulders, walked down the steps and across the schoolyard.

6 The Real Mr. Jenkins

"Charles!" Meg cried.

All three Mr. Jenkinses held up warning hands, said simultaneously, "Charles Wallace Murry, what is it *now?*"

Charles Wallace looked with interest at the three men. "Hello, what's this?"

Mr. Jenkins One said, "What are you doing with that— that—"

All three men were visibly fearful of Louise. There was no telling the 'real' Mr. Jenkins by a variation in response to the snake. Louise reared her head, half closed her eyes, and made the strange, clacking, warning sound which Meg had heard the night before. Charles Wallace stroked her soothingly, and looked speculatively at the three men.

"We were supposed to bring a small pet to school today, to share with the class."

Meg thought, —Good for you, Charles, to think of Louise the Larger. If you terrified Mr. Jenkins, that would send you up a notch in the other kids' estimation. If there's one thing everybody in school agrees on, it's that Mr. Jenkins is a retarded rodent.

Mr. Jenkins Three said severely, "You know perfectly well that *small* pets were meant, Charles Wallace. Turtles or tropical fish or perhaps even a hamster."

109

"Or a gerbil," Mr. Jenkins Two added. "A gerbil would be acceptable."

"Why have you multiplied?" Charles Wallace asked. "I found one of you quite enough."

Louise clacked again; it was a flesh-chilling sound.

Mr. Jenkins Three demanded, "Why aren't you in class, Charles?"

"Because the teacher told me to take Louise the Larger and go home. I really don't understand why. Louise is friendly and she wouldn't hurt anybody. Only the girls were scared of her. She lives in our stone wall by the twins' vegetable garden."

Meg looked at Louise, at the hooded eyes, the wary position of the head, the warning twitching of the last few inches of her black tail. Blajeny had told them that Louise was a Teacher. Louise herself had certainly shown in the past twenty-four hours that she was more than an ordinary garden snake. Louise would know—did know, Meg was sure —the real Mr. Jenkins. Swallowing her own shyness of all snakes, she reached out towards Charles Wallace. "Let me have Louise for a little while, please, Charles."

But Proginoskes spoke in her mind. "No, Meg. You have to do it yourself. You can't let Louise do it for you."

All right. She accepted that. But perhaps Louise could still help.

Charles Wallace regarded his sister thoughtfully. Then he held out the arm around which Louise's lower half was coiled. The snake slithered sinuously to Meg. Her body felt cold, and tingled with electricity. Meg tried not to flinch.

"Mr. Jenkins," Meg said. "Each of you. One at a time.

What are you going to do about Charles Wallace and Louise? Charles Wallace can't possibly walk home alone. It's too far. What are you going to do about Charles Wallace and school in general?"

Nobody volunteered an answer. All three folded their arms impassively across their chests.

"Mr. Jenkins Three," Meg said.

"Are you Naming me, Meg? That's right."

"I'm not Naming anybody yet. I want to know what you're going to do."

"I thought I had already told you. It is a situation which I shall have to guide carefully. It was foolish of Charlie to bring a snake to school. Snakes are quite frightening to some people, you know."

Louise hissed slowly. Mr. Jenkins Three turned visibly paler.

He said, "I shall have a long, quiet session with Charles Wallace's teacher. Then I will speak to each child in the first-grade room, separately. I shall see to it that each one has an understanding of the problem. If any of them group together and try bullying, I shall use strong disciplinary methods. This school has been run in far too lax and permissive a manner. From now on, I intend to hold the reins. And now, Charles Wallace, I shall drive you home. Your sister will bring your pet."

Meg turned away from him. "Mr. Jenkins Two?"

Mr. Jenkins Two detached himself by one pace from the others. "Force, that's what that impostor is advocating. Dictatorship. I will never put up with a dictatorship. But you should not have brought the snake to school, Charlie. You should have known better. But I think I understand. You thought it would enhance your social prestige, and make you more of an equal in the eyes of your peers. There's where happiness lies, in success with your peer group. I want all my children to be like each other, so we must help you to be more normal, even if it means that you must go to school elsewhere for a while. I understand there's someone from another galaxy who's interested in helping you. Perhaps that's our answer for the time being."

Meg turned to Mr. Jenkins One. He gave a small, annoyed, Mr. Jenkins shrug. "I really do not foresee much change in my relationship with Charles Wallace in the future. Why interplanetary travel should be thought of as a solution to all earth's problems I do not understand. We have sent men to the moon and to Mars and we are none the better for it. Why sending Charles Wallace a few billion light-years across space should improve him any, I fail to see. Unless, of course, it helps his physical condition, about which nobody except myself appears concerned." He looked at his wristwatch. "How much longer does this farce continue?"

Meg could feel sharp, painful little flickers as the cherubim thought at her. She did not want to listen.

"It's all a waste of time!" she cried. "Why do I have to bother with all these Mr. Jenkinses? What can it possibly have to do with Charles?"

Louise the Larger's breath was cool and gentle against her ear. "It doess, it doess," the snake hissed.

Proginoskes said, "You don't need to know why. Just get on with it."

Charles Wallace spoke wearily. "Give me Louise, please, Meg. I want to go home."

"It's too far for you to walk."

"We'll take it slowly."

Mr. Jenkins Three said sharply, "I have already said I will drive you home. You may take the snake as long as it stays in the back seat."

Mr. Jenkins One and Two said simultaneously, "*I* will drive Charles Wallace. And the snake." They shuddered slightly, not quite simultaneously, but in syncopation.

Charles Wallace held out his arm and Louise slithered from Meg to the little boy. "Let's go," he said to the three men, turned away from them, and started to walk to where the faculty parked their cars. The Mr. Jenkinses followed him, walking abreast, all with the stiff, ungainly gait which was distinctively and solely Mr. Jenkins.

"But who will he go with?" Meg asked Proginoskes.

"The real one."

"But then—"

"I think that when they turn the corner there'll be only one of them. It gives us a small respite, at any rate." The cherubim materialized slowly, becoming at first a shimmer, then a transparent outline, then deepening in dimensions until he moved into complete visibility as the three Mr. Jenkinses disappeared. "Don't waste time," he thought sharply at her. "Think. What's the nicest thing you've ever heard about Mr. Jenkins?"

"Nice? Nothing nice. Listen, maybe all of them are impostors. Maybe they won't come back."

Again the sharp little pain. "That's too easy. One of

them's real, and for some reason he's important. Think, Meg. You must know something good about him."

"I don't want to know anything good about him."

"Stop thinking about yourself. Think about Charles. The real Mr. Jenkins can help Charles."

"How?"

"We don't need to know how, Meg! Stop blocking me. It's our only hope. You must let me kythe with you." She felt him moving about within her mind, more gently now, but persistently. "You're still blocking me."

"I'm trying not to—"

"I know. Do some math problems in your head. Anything to shut out your un-love and let me in about Mr. Jenkins. Do some math for Calvin. You love Calvin. Good. Think about Calvin. Meg! Calvin's shoes."

"What about them?"

"What kind of shoes does he have on?"

"His regular school shoes, I suppose. How would I know? I think he has only one pair of shoes, and his sneakers."

"What are the shoes like?"

"I don't know. I didn't notice. I don't bother much about clothes."

"Think some more math and let me show them to you."

Shoes. Strong, fairly new Oxfords which Calvin wore over mismated red and purple socks, the kind of shoes Mr. O'Keefe could ill afford to buy for his family. Meg saw the shoes vividly; the image was given her by Proginoskes; she had been quite truthful when she told him that she didn't notice clothes. Nevertheless, her mind registered all that she saw and it was there, stored, available to the kything of the cherubim. She saw with a flash of intuition that her kything was like a small child's trying to pick out a melody on the piano with one finger, as against the harmony of a full orchestra, like the cherubic language.

In her mind's ear came the echo of Calvin's voice, coming back to her from an afternoon when she had been sent—unfairly, she thought—to Mr. Jenkins's office, and been dealt with—unfairly—there. Calvin's voice, quiet, calming, infuriatingly reasonable. "When I started seventh grade and went over to Regional, my mother bought me some shoes from a thrift shop. They cost her a dollar, which was more than she could spare, and they were women's Oxfords, the kind of black laced shoes old women wear, and at least three sizes too small for me. When I saw them, I cried, and then my mother cried. And my pop beat me. So I got a saw and hacked off the heels, and cut the toes out so I could jam my feet in, and went to school. The kids knew me too well to make remarks in my presence, but I could guess what they were sniggering behind my back. After a few days Mr. Jenkins called me into his office and said he'd noticed I'd outgrown my shoes, and he just happened to have an extra pair he thought would fit me. He'd gone to a lot of trouble to make them look used, as though he hadn't gone out and bought them for me. I make enough money in the summers now to buy my own shoes, but I'll never forget that he gave me the first decent pair of shoes I ever had. Sure I know all the bad things about him, and they're all true, and I've had my own run-ins with him, but on the whole we get along, maybe because my parents don't make him feel inferior, and he knows he can do things for me that they can't."

Meg muttered, "It'd have been a lot easier if I could have gone on hating him."

Now it was Proginoskes's voice in her mind's ear, not Calvin's. "What would be easier?"

"Naming him."

"Would it? Don't you know more about him now?"

"Second-hand. I've never known him to do anything else nice."

"How do you suppose he feels about you?"

"He's never seen me except when I'm snarly," she admitted. She found herself almost laughing as she remembered Mr. Jenkins saying, 'Margaret, you are the most contumacious child it has ever been my misfortune to have in this office,' and she had had to go home and look up 'contumacious.'

Proginoskes probed, "Do you think he'd believe anything good about you?"

"Not likely."

"Would you like him to see a different Meg? The real Meg?"

She shrugged.

"Well, then, how would you like to be different with him?"

Frantically, she said, "I wish I had gorgeous blond hair."

"You wouldn't, not really."

"Of course I would!"

"If you had gorgeous blond hair, you wouldn't be you."

"That might be a good idea. Ouch, Progo, you hurt!"

"This isn't any time for self-indulgence."

"When Mr. Jenkins is being nice, he's not being Mr. Jenkins. Being nice on Mr. Jenkins would be like blond hair on me."

Proginoskes sent ice-cold anger through her. "Meg, there's no more time. They'll be back any moment now."

Panic churned in her. "Progo, if I don't Name right, if I fail, what will you do?"

"I told you. I have to choose."

"That's not telling me. I want to know which way you're going to choose."

Proginoskes's feathers shivered as though a cold wind had blown through them. "Meg, there isn't much time. They're on their way back. You have to Name one of them."

"Give me a hint."

"This isn't a game. Mr. Jenkins was right."

She shot him an anguished glance, and he lowered several sets of eyelashes in apology. "Progo, even for Charles Wallace, how can I do the impossible? How can I love Mr. Jenkins?"

Proginoskes did not respond. There was no flame, no smoke; only a withdrawing of eyes behind wings.

"Progo! Help me! How can I feel love for Mr. Jenkins?"

Immediately he opened a large number of eyes very wide. "What a strange idea. Love isn't *feeling*. If it were, I wouldn't be able to love. Cherubim don't have feelings."

"But—"

117

"Idiot," Proginoskes said, anxiously rather than crossly. "Love isn't how you feel. It's what you do. I've never had a feeling in my life. As a matter of fact, I matter only with earth people."

"Progo, you matter to me."

Proginoskes puffed enveloping pale blue clouds. "That's not what I meant. I meant that cherubim only *matter* with earth people. You call it materializing."

"Then, if you become visible only for us, why do you have to look so terrifying?"

"Because when we matter, this is how we come out. When you got mattered, you didn't choose to look the way you do, did you?"

"I certainly did not. I'd have chosen quite differently. I'd have chosen to be beautiful—oh, I see! You mean you don't have any more choice about looking like a drive of deformed dragons than I do about my hair and glasses and everything? You aren't doing it this way just for fun?"

Proginoskes held three of its wings demurely over a great many of its eyes. "I am a cherubim, and when a cherubim takes on matter, this is how."

Meg knelt in front of the great, frightening, and strangely beautiful creature. "Progo, I'm not a wind or a flame of fire. I'm a human being. I feel. I can't think without feeling. If you matter to me, then what you decide to do if I fail matters."

"I fail to see why."

She scrambled to her feet, batting at the last wisps of pale blue smoke which stung her eyes, and shouted, "Because if you decide to turn into a worm or whatever and join the Echthroi, I don't care whether I Name right or not! It just doesn't matter to me! And Charles Wallace would feel the same way—I know he would!"

Proginoskes probed gently and thoughtfully into her mind. "I don't understand your feelings. I'm trying to, but I don't. It must be extremely unpleasant to have feelings."

"Progo! What will you do?"

Silence. No flame. No smoke. All eyes closed. Proginoskes folded the great wings completely. His words were very small as they moved into her mind. "X. If you fail, I will X myself."

He vanished.

Meg swung around and three Mr. Jenkinses were walking towards her from the direction of the parking lot. She faced them. "Mr. Jenkins."

Identical, hateful, simultaneous, they stepped towards her.

Mr. Jenkins One sniffed, the end of his pink nose wriggling distastefully. "I am back. I left Charles Wallace with your mother. Now will you please get rid of these two—uh —pranksters. I resent this intrusion on my time and privacy."

Mr. Jenkins Two pointed to One accusingly. "That impostor lost his temper and showed his true colors when your little brother brought his snake to school. The impostor forgot himself and called the child a sn—"

"Delete," Mr. Jenkins Three said sharply. "He used words unsuitable for a child. Blip it."

119

Mr. Jenkins Two said, "He doesn't love children."

Mr. Jenkins Three said, "He can't control children."

Mr. Jenkins Two said, "I will make Charles Wallace happy."

Mr. Jenkins Three said, "I will make him successful."

Mr. Jenkins One looked at his watch.

Meg closed her eyes. And suddenly she did not feel. She had been pushed into a dimension beyond feeling, if such a thing is possible, and if Progo was right, it is possible. There was nothing but a cold awareness which had nothing to do with what she normally would have thought of as feeling. Her voice issued from her lips almost without volition, cold, calm, emotionless. "Mr. Jenkins Three—"

He stepped forward, smiling triumphantly.

"No. You're not the real Mr. Jenkins. You're much too powerful. You'd never have to be taken away from a regional school you couldn't control and made principal of a grade school you couldn't control, either." She looked at Mr. Jenkins One and Two. Her hands were ice-cold and she had the sensation in the pit of the stomach which precedes acute nausea, but she was unaware of this because she was still in the strange realm beyond feeling. "Mr. Jenkins Two—"

He smiled.

Again she shook her head. "I wasn't quite as sure about you at first. But wanting to make everybody happy and just like everybody else is just as bad as Mr. Jenkins Three manipulating everybody. Bad as Mr. Jenkins is, he's the only one of the three of you who's human enough to make as many mistakes as he does, and that's you, Mr. Jenkins One—" Suddenly she gave a startled laugh. "And I do love you for it." Then she burst into tears of nervousness and exhaustion. But she had no doubt that she was right.

The air about the schoolyard was rent with a great howling and shrieking and then a cold nothingness which could only be the presence of Echthroi. It was as though rip after rip were being slashed in the air, and then the edges were drawn together and healed.

Silence. And quiet. And a small, ordinary, everyday wind.

Proginoskes materialized, delicately unfolding wing after wing to reveal his myriad various eyes.

Mr. Jenkins One, the real Mr. Jenkins, fainted.

7 Metron Ariston

Meg bent over Mr. Jenkins. She did not realize that Blajeny was there until she heard his voice.

"Really, Proginoskes, you ought to know better than to take anyone by surprise like that, particularly a still-limited one like Mr. Jenkins." He stood between the cherubim and Meg, almost as tall as the school building, half amused, half angry.

Proginoskes fluttered several wings in halfhearted apology. "I was very relieved."

"Quite."

"Will this—uh—Mr. Jenkins ever be anything but a limited one?"

"That is a limited and limiting thought, Proginoskes," Blajeny said sternly. "I am surprised."

Now the cherubim was truly abashed. He closed his eyes and covered them with wings, keeping only three eyes open, one each to gaze at Blajeny, Meg, and the prone Mr. Jenkins.

Blajeny turned to Meg. "My child, I am very pleased with you."

Meg blushed. "Shouldn't we do something about Mr. Jenkins?"

Blajeny knelt on the dusty ground. His dark fingers, with their vast span, pressed gently against Mr. Jenkins's temples;

the principal's usually pasty face was grey; his body gave a spasmodic twitch; he opened his eyes and closed them again immediately; moaned.

Tension and relief had set Meg on the verge of hysteria; she was half laughing, half crying. "Blajeny, don't you realize you must be almost as frightening to poor Mr. Jenkins as Progo?" She, too, dropped to her knees beside the principal. "Mr. Jenkins, I'm here. Meg. I know you don't like me, but at least I'm familiar. Open your eyes. It's all right. Really it is."

Slowly, cautiously, he opened his eyes. "I must make an appointment with a psychiatrist. Immediately."

Meg spoke soothingly, as to a very small child. "You aren't hallucinating, Mr. Jenkins, honestly you aren't. It's all right. They're friends, Blajeny and Progo. And they're real."

Mr. Jenkins closed his eyes, opened them again, focused on Meg.

"Blajeny is a Teacher, Mr. Jenkins, and Progo is a— well, he's a cherubim." She could hardly blame Mr. Jenkins for looking incredulous.

His voice was thin. "Either I am in the process of a nervous breakdown, which is not unlikely, or I am dreaming. That's it. I must be asleep." He struggled to sit up, with Meg's assistance. "But why, then, are you in my dream? Why am I lying on the ground? Has somebody hit me? I wouldn't put it past the bigger boys—" He rubbed his hand over his head, searching for a bruise. "Why are you here, Margaret? I seem to remember—" He looked once more at Blajeny and Proginoskes and shuddered. "They're still here. No. I am still dreaming. Why can't I wake up? This isn't real."

Meg echoed Blajeny. "What is real?" She turned to the Teacher, but he was no longer paying attention to Mr. Jenkins. She followed Blajeny's gaze, and saw Louise slithering rapidly towards them.

A fresh shudder shook Mr. Jenkins. "Not the snake again —I have a phobia about—"

Meg soothed, "Louise is really very friendly. She won't hurt you."

"Snakes." Mr. Jenkins shook his head. "Snakes and monsters and giants . . . It's not possible, none of this is possible . . ."

Blajeny turned from his conversation with Louise the Larger, spoke urgently. "We must go at once. The Echthroi are enraged. Charles Wallace's mitochondritis is now acute."

"Oh, Blajeny, take us home quickly," Meg cried. "I must be with him!"

"There isn't time. We must go at once to Metron Ariston."

"Where?"

Without answering, Blajeny turned from Meg to Mr. Jenkins. "You, sir: do you wish to return to your school and continue your regular day's work? Or will you throw in your lot with us?"

Mr. Jenkins looked completely bewildered. "I am having a nervous breakdown."

"You don't need to have one if you don't want to. You have simply been faced with several things outside your current spheres of experience. That does not mean that they—we—do not exist."

Meg felt an unwilling sense of protectiveness towards this unattractive little man she had Named. "Mr. Jenkins, don't you think you'd better report that you're not well today, and come with us?"

Mr. Jenkins held out his hands helplessly. "Were there —there were—two other—two men who resembled me?"

"Yes, of course there were. But they've gone."

"Where?"

Meg turned to Blajeny.

The Teacher looked grave. "When an Echthros takes on a human body, it tends to keep it."

Meg caught hold of the stone grey of the Teacher's sleeve. "The first test—how did it happen? You didn't make it up, did you? You couldn't have told the Echthroi to turn into Mr. Jenkins, could you?"

"Meg," he replied quietly, "I told you I needed your help."

"You mean—you mean this was going to happen, anyhow, the Echthroi turning into Mr. Jenkins, even if—"

"Mr. Jenkins was a perfect host for their purposes."

Rather shakily, Mr. Jenkins tottered towards Blajeny, sputtering, "Now, see here, I don't know who you are and I don't care, but I demand an explanation."

Blajeny's voice was now more like an English horn than a cello. "Perhaps in your world today such a phenomenon would be called schizophrenia. I prefer the old idea of possession."

"Schiz—are you, sir, questioning my sanity?"

125

Louise's small voice whistled urgently.

"Mr. Jenkins," Blajeny said quietly, "we must leave. Either return to your school or come with us. Now."

To Meg's surprise she found herself urging, "Please come with us, Mr. Jenkins."

"But my duty—"

"You know you can't just go back to school again after what's happened."

Mr. Jenkins moaned again. His complexion had turned from grey to pale green.

"And after you've met the cherubim and Blajeny—"

"Cheru—"

Louise whistled again.

Blajeny asked, "Are you coming with us or not?"

"Margaret Named me," Mr. Jenkins said softly. "Yes. I will come."

Proginoskes reached out a great pinion and pulled Meg in to him. She felt the tremendous heartbeat, a beat which reverberated like a brass gong. Then she saw the ovoid eye, open, dilating . . .

She was through.

It was something of an anticlimax to find that they were no farther from home than the star-watching rock.

Wait: was it, after all, the star-watching rock?

She blinked, and when she opened her eyes Mr. Jenkins and Blajeny were there, and Calvin was there, too (oh, thank you, Blajeny!), holding his hand out to her, and she was warmed in the radiance of his big smile.

It was no longer autumn-cold. There was a light breeze, warm and summery. All about them, encircling them, was the sound of summer insects, crickets, katydids, and—less pleasantly—the shrill of a mosquito. Frogs were crunking away, and a tree toad sang its scratchy song. The sky was thick with stars, stars which always seemed closer to earth in summer than in winter.

Blajeny sat down, cross-legged, on the rock, and beckoned to them. Meg sat in front of him, and saw that Louise was coiled nearby, her head resting on one of Proginoskes's outstretched wings. Calvin sat beside Meg, and Mr. Jenkins stood awkwardly, shifting his weight from one leg to the other.

Meg moved a little closer to Calvin and looked up at the sky.

And gasped. The stars, the low, daisy-thick summer stars, were not the familiar planets and constellations she had so often watched with her parents. They were as different as had been the constellations where Proginoskes had taken her to see the terrible work of the Echthroi.

"Blajeny," Calvin asked, "where are we?"

"Metron Ariston."

"What's Metron Ariston? Is it a planet?"

"No. It's an idea, a postulatum. I find it easier to posit when I am in my home galaxy, so we are near the Mondrion solar system of the Veganuel galaxy. The stars you see are those I know, those which I see from my home planet."

"Why are we here?"

127

"The postulatum Metron Ariston makes it possible for all sizes to become relative. Within Metron Ariston you may be sized so that you are able to converse with a giant star or a tiny farandola."

Meg felt a moment of shock and disbelief. Farandolae were still less real to her than Charles Wallace's 'dragons.' "A farandola! Are we really going to see one?"

"Yes."

"But it's impossible. A farandola is so small that—"

"How small is it?" Blajeny asked.

"So small that it's beyond rational conceiving, my mother says."

Mr. Jenkins made a small confused noise and shifted weight again. Blajeny said, "And yet Mrs. Murry is convinced that she has proved the existence of farandolae. Now let us suppose: here we are in Veganuel galaxy, two trillion light-years away. Veganuel is just about the same size as your own Earth's galaxy. How long does it take the Milky Way to rotate once around?"

As no one else spoke, Meg answered, "Two hundred billion years, clockwise."

"So that gives us a general idea of the size of your galaxy, doesn't it?"

"Very general," Calvin said. "Our minds can't comprehend anything that huge, that macrocosmic."

"Don't try to comprehend with your mind. Your minds are very limited. Use your intuition. Think of the size of your galaxy. Now, think of your sun. It's a star, and it is a great deal smaller than the entire galaxy, isn't it?"

"Of course."

"Think of yourselves, now, in comparison with the size of your sun. Think how much smaller you are. Have you done that?"

"Sort of," Meg said.

"Now think of a mitochondrion. Think of the mitochondria which live in the cells of all living things, and how much smaller a mitochondrion is than you."

Mr. Jenkins said, to himself, "I thought Charles Wallace was making them up to show off."

Blajeny continued, "Now consider that a farandola is as much smaller than a mitochondrion as a mitochondrion is smaller than you are."

"This time," Calvin said, "the problem is that our minds can't comprehend anything that *micro*cosmic."

Blajeny said, "Another way of putting it would be to say that a farandola is as much smaller than you are as your galaxy is larger than you are."

Calvin whistled. "Then, to a farandola, any of us would be as big as a galaxy?"

"More or less. You *are* a galaxy for your farandolae."

"Then how can we possibly meet one?"

Blajeny's voice was patient. "I have just told you that in Metron Ariston we can almost do away with variations in size, which are, in reality, quite unimportant." He turned his head and looked in the direction of the great glacial rocks.

"The rocks," Meg asked, "are they really there?"

"Nothing is anywhere in Metron Ariston," Blajeny said.

"I am trying to make things as easy for you as I can by giving you a familiar visual setting. You must try to understand things not only with your little human minds, which are not a great deal of use in the problems which confront us."

At last Mr. Jenkins sat, crouching uncomfortably on the rock. "With what can I understand, then? I don't have very much intuition."

"You must understand with your hearts. With the whole of yourselves, not just a fragment."

Mr. Jenkins groaned. "I am too old to be educable. You can't teach an old dog new tricks. I have lived beyond my time."

Meg cried, "Oh, no, you haven't, Mr. Jenkins, you're just beginning!"

Mr. Jenkins shook his head in mournful negation. "Maybe it would have been better if you'd never Named me. Why did I ever have to see you this way? Or your little brother? Or that frightful beast?"

Proginoskes made what seemed like a minor volcanic upheaval.

Mr. Jenkins stiffened a little, though he could hardly become paler. "Are there any more like you?"

"There are a goodly number of cherubim," Proginoskes replied, "but none exactly alike."

"That's it," Mr. Jenkins said. "That's precisely it." Absent-mindedly he brushed at the dandruff and lint on the shoulders of his dark suit.

Blajeny, listening carefully, bowed his great head courteously. "Precisely what, Mr. Jenkins?"

"Nobody should be exactly like anybody else."

"Is anybody?"

"Those—those—imitation Mr. Jenkinses—to see myself doubled and trebled—there's nothing left to hold on to."

Impulsively Meg got up and ran to the principal. "But they aren't like you, Mr. Jenkins! Nobody is! You *are* unique. I Named you, didn't I?"

Mr. Jenkins's eyes looked blurred and bewildered through the lenses of his spectacles. "Yes. Yes, you did. I suppose that's why I'm here—wherever here is." He turned to Blajeny. "Those other Mr. Jenkinses—you called them Echthroi?"

"Yes. The Echthroi are those who hate, those who would keep you from being Named, who would un-Name you. It is the nature of love to create. It is the nature of hate to destroy."

Mr. Jenkins said, heavily, "I fear I have not been a loving person."

Meg felt a flash of intuition as sharp and brilliant as the cherubim's flame; like flame, it burned. "Oh, Mr. Jenkins, don't you see? Every time I was in your office, being awful and hating you, I was really hating myself more than you. Mother was right. She told me that you underestimate yourself."

Mr. Jenkins responded in a strange voice she had never heard from him before, completely unlike his usual, nasal,

131

shrill asperity. "We both do, don't we, Margaret? When I thought your parents were looking down on me, I was really looking down on myself. But I don't see any other way to look at myself."

Now at last Meg glimpsed the Mr. Jenkins who had bought shoes for Calvin, who had clumsily tried to make those shoes look worn.

Mr. Jenkins turned to Blajeny. "These Echth—"

"Echthroi. Singular, Echthros."

"These Echthroi who took on—who took on my likeness," Mr. Jenkins said, "can they cause more trouble?"

"Yes."

"They would harm Charles Wallace?"

"They would X—extinguish him," the cherubim said.

Meg reached out in longing and fear towards her brother. "We shouldn't have left him—" she started, then closed her mouth. She felt the cherubim moving gently within her, helping her, giving her little shoves of thought, and then she seemed to be with Charles Wallace, not in actuality, not in person, but in her heart. In her heart's sight she saw their mother carrying him up the stairs, Charles limp in his mother's arms, legs dangling. Mrs. Murry went into his room, a small, paneled room with a little fireplace, and one wall papered in a blue and white snowflake pattern, a safe, comfortable room. The window looked out onto the pine woods behind the house; the light which came in was gentle, and kind.

Mrs. Murry laid Charles Wallace down on his bed, and began to undress him. The child barely had the strength to help her; he made an effort to smile and said, "I'll be better soon. Meg will . . ."

"Meg will be home from school in a couple of hours," their mother said. "She'll be right up to see you. And Dr. Louise is on her way."

"Meg isn't—in school." Speaking was almost too great an effort.

Mrs. Murry did not contradict him, as perhaps she might have normally, but helped him into his pajamas.

"I'm cold, Mother."

She pulled the covers up over him. "I'll get another blanket."

A sound of feet pounding up the stairs, and the twins burst in:

"What's this? What's the matter?"

"Is Charles sick?"

Mrs. Murry answered quietly, "He's not feeling very well."

"Bad enough to go to bed?"

"Did he have trouble in school again?"

"School was fine. He took Louise and she made a great hit, evidently."

"Our Louise?"

"Louise the Larger?"

"Yes."

"Bully for you, Charles!"

"That's telling them!"

Charles Wallace managed a reasonably good smile.

"Sandy," Mrs. Murry said, "please bring up some wood

for a fire. It's a little chilly. Dennys, if you'd please go to the cedar closet and get another blanket . . ."

"Okay. Sure. Right away."

"And Meg'll read to you or something when she gets home, Charles."

Meg thought she heard Charles Wallace saying once again that Meg was not in school, but it was as though a mist swept over the vivid scene, and Charles Wallace's room was gone, and Meg was standing, pressed close against the cherubim, who had one wing strongly about her.

Blajeny said, "Now, my children, we must have a lesson. Let us make believe that it is daytime. You can, you know. Believing takes practice, but neither you, Calvin, nor you, Meg, is old enough to have forgotten completely how to do it. You must make believe for yourselves and for Mr. Jenkins. This may seem a trivial task, in view of the gravity of the circumstances, but it is practice for what is to come. Now. Make believe. Turn night to day."

The cherubim withdrew his wing and Meg put her hand in Blajeny's. Her own hand was very small in comparison, as small as it had been when she was younger than Charles Wallace and had held her father's hand in complete love and trust. She looked up at Blajeny's grave, black face, looked into the strange amber eyes which sometimes seemed to hold the cold light of the moon, and which now glowed with the warmth of the sun. Color flooded the imaged sky of Metron Ariston, a vast, arching blue canopy, cloudless, and shimmering with warmth. About the rock the green grasses of summer rippled in the breeze; a bird sang, was joined by another, others, until melody was all around them. The grass was brightened by field flowers, daisies, black-eyed Susans, Indian paintbrushes, butter-and-eggs, purple thistles, all the summer flowers blooming abundantly and brilliantly.

Colors blazed more brightly than normal. Calvin's hair, the shade of an Indian paintbrush, burned like sunlight. His freckles seemed larger and more profuse than ever. The faded blue of his jacket had deepened to meet the gentian blue of his eyes. He had on one red sock and one purple sock.

Meg's old kilt, faded from countless washings, looked bright and new, but her hair, she thought, was probably as mouse-brown as ever; and Mr. Jenkins was still pasty and colorless. Louise the Larger, however, looked even larger than usual, and her coils shone with purple and gold.

Meg looked towards Proginoskes and the shining of the cherubim was so brilliant it almost blinded her; she had to look away.

"Now, my children," Blajeny said, and he included Mr. Jenkins in the appellation, "we will welcome the other member of this class."

From behind the smaller of the two glacial rocks a tiny creature appeared and scampered over to them. It looked rather like a small, silver-blue mouse, and yet it seemed to Meg to be a sea creature rather than a land creature. Its ears were large and velvety, the fur shading off into lavender fringes at the tips, blowing gently in the breeze like sea plants moving in the currents of the ocean. Its whiskers were unusually long; its eyes were large and milky and had no visible pupil or iris, but there was nothing dulled about them; they shone like moonstones.

It spoke, but with neither a mouse's squeak nor a human voice. The sound was like harp strings being plucked under water, and the long whiskers vibrated almost as though they were being played. It did not give forth words, and yet it was quite plain that it was saying something like "Hello, are you my classmates?"

Blajeny spoke in the mouse-creature's language; words did not issue from his mouth; his granite lips were closed; and yet the children heard the lovely rippling harp sound.

The mouse-creature did not seem pleased, and made sounds which conveyed a good deal of doubt. Meg understood it to be complaining that if it had to pass even the most preliminary of examinations with an earthling, it was dubious that it could do so. A cherubim might be of some help, but surely earthlings were nothing but—

Proginoskes said, "I, too, had misgivings about earthlings. But the girl earthling and I have just come through the first ordeal, and it was the girl who did it."

The mouse-creature's whiskers twingled. "It can't have been much of an ordeal. Can we please get going, Blajeny? We have only a parsec before I make my preliminary report. And I can see I have a great deal to teach whomever I'm unfortunate enough to have as a partner—even if it's the cherubim." Its long, lavender tail, which had a fish-like fan at the tip, switched, and its whiskers bristled in Meg's direction.

Meg bristled, too. "Perhaps when I'm as old as you are I'll have learned a few things to teach *you!*"

Mouse-creature's whiskers vibrated wildly. "Age is immaterial. In any case, it so happens that I was born only yesterday."

"Then what are you doing here?"

Mouse-creature drew itself up; now it reminded Meg not so much of a mouse as of a small shrimp with antennae waving wildly. "There's only one of us farandolae born every generation or so nowadays, and we start our schooling the moment we're born."

"You're a farandola!"

"Naturally. What did you expect me to be? What else could I possibly be? Everybody knows that the farandolae—"

She interrupted. "Everybody doesn't. The existence of farandolae wasn't even guessed at until a few years ago when we began to learn more about mitochondria, and my mother has just now isolated the effect of farandolae on mitochondria with her micro-sonarscope. And even with the micro-electron microscope, farandolae can just be proved to exist, they can't really be seen."

The mouse-creature's, the farandola's, whiskers twanged. "It's a very stupid breed of creature that doesn't know its own inhabitants. Especially if it's fortunate enough to be inhabited by farandolae. We are extremely important and getting more so."

Past the farandola, behind Proginoskes and Louise the

137

Larger, the shape of a Mr. Jenkins blew rapidly across the horizon.

Mr. Jenkins, standing near Meg and Calvin, quivered.

Blajeny looked grim. "Echthroi at work."

The mouse-creature-farandola paid no attention. "My quercus, my tree, hasn't had an offspring for a hundred years—our years, of course. It will take me that long to become full-grown myself, and this is only my second phase."

Meg spoke in her most ungracious manner. "You're going to tell us about your first phase whether we want you to or not. So go ahead." The glimpse of Charles Wallace, followed by the sight of another Echthros-Mr. Jenkins, had forced her to realize that the successful passing of the first test did not mean that everything was going to be all right.

Mouse-shrimp-farandola reacted by an intensified trembling of feelers. "Yesterday morning I was still contained inside the single golden fruit hanging on my tree. At noon it burst and fell open, and there was I, newly hatched. In my tadpole stage I was delivered to Metron Ariston and transmogrified, and here am I. My name is Sporos, by the way, and I do not like your thinking names like mouse-creature and shrimp-thing at me. *Sporos.* When I have finished this phase of my education—if I finish—with one of you for a partner, I will root myself, and Deepen. After an aeon I'll send up a small green shoot out of my kelp bed, and start growing into an aqueous deciduous spore-reproducing fruit-bearing coniferous farandola."

138

Calvin looked horrified. "You're mad. I've studied biology. You're not possible."

"Neither are you," Sporos replied indignantly. "Nothing *important* is. Blajeny, is it my misfortune to be paired with one of these earthlings?"

Louise the Larger lifted her head out of her coils and looked at Sporos, her heavy lids met and closed.

Blajeny said, "You are hardly making yourself popular, Sporos."

"I'm not a mere earthling. Earthlings are important only because they are inhabited by farandolae. Popularity is immaterial to farandolae."

Blajeny turned away from Sporos in quiet rebuff. "Calvin. You and Sporos are to work together."

"Oh, well, you can't win them all," was more or less the effect of what Sporos was vibrating, and Meg thought it would have been a more appropriate response coming from Calvin.

Mr. Jenkins said, "Blajeny, if I may presume—"

"Yes?"

"That other—I did see another copy of myself just a few moments ago, did I not?"

"Yes. I am afraid you did."

"What does it mean?"

Blajeny said, "It means nothing good."

Proginoskes added, "You see, we aren't any place. We're in Metron Ariston. We're simply in an idea which Blajeny happens to be having in the middle of the Mondrion solar

139

system in Veganuel galaxy. An Echthros-Mr. Jenkins oughtn't to be able to follow us here. It means—"

"What?" Meg demanded.

Like Blajeny, Proginoskes said, "Nothing good."

Sporos twingled his whiskers. "Need we stand around chittering? When are we going?"

"Very soon."

"Where?" Meg demanded. She felt prickles of foreboding.

"To a far place, Meg."

"But Mother and Father—Charles Wallace—the twins —we can't just go off this way with Charles Wallace so ill and—"

"That is why we are going, Meg," Blajeny said.

Sporos rippled his undulating notes, and Meg translated something like: "Can't you just call home, or just reach out and talk to each other when you want to?" and then a horrified, "Oh, my goodness, I don't see how anybody as ignorant as you three earthlings seem to be can possibly manage. Do you mean on your earth host you never communicate with each other and with other planets? You mean your planet revolves about all isolated in space? Aren't you terribly lonely? Isn't he?"

"He?"

"Or she. Your planet. Aren't you lonely?"

"Maybe we are, a little," Calvin conceded. "But it's a beautiful planet."

"That," Sporos said, "is as it may be. Since I was only born yesterday and came right into Metron Ariston and to Blajeny, I don't know the planets except the ones in the Mondrion solar system, and they talk back and forth all the time; they chatter too much, if you ask me."

"We didn't," Meg tried to interrupt, but Sporos twingled on.

"I do hope I wasn't born in some dreadful mitochondrion which lives in some horrible isolated human host on a lonely planet like yours. You *are* all from the same planet? I thought so. Oh dear, oh dear, I can see you aren't going to be the least help to me in passing any of the trials. I'd better see what time it is."

"How do you tell time?" Calvin asked curiously.

"By the leaves, of course. You mean to say you don't even know the time of day?"

"Of course I do. With my watch."

"What's a watch?"

Calvin extended his wrist. He was very proud of his watch, which had been a prize at school, and gave the date as well as the hour, had a sweep hand, and was a stop watch as well.

"What a peculiar object." Sporos regarded it with a certain contempt. "Does it work just for your time, or for time in general?"

"Just for our time, I guess."

"You mean, if you want to know what time it is anywhere here in Blajeny's galaxy, or in a distant mitochondrion, your watch thing won't tell you?"

"Well—no. It just tells the time for whatever time zone I'm in."

"Mighty Yadah! How confused everything must be on your planet. I only hope my human host isn't in your planet."

Mr. Jenkins said plaintively, "If someone would just explain to me what is going on—"

"Mr. Jenkins," Meg said. "You know what the Echthroi are—"

"But I don't. I only know that they impersonated me."

Blajeny placed both great hands on Mr. Jenkins's stooped shoulders and looked down at him gravely. "There are evil forces at work in the world."

Mr. Jenkins nodded mutely. He did not dispute that.

"They are throughout the universe."

Mr. Jenkins glanced at the cherubim, who had stretched out his wings to their fullest span as though to flex his muscles. "How—how big are they?"

"They are no size and they are every size. An Echthros can be as large as a galaxy and as small as a farandola. Or, as you have seen, a replica of yourself. They are the powers of nothingness, those who would un-Name. Their aim is total X—to extinguish all creation."

"What do they have to do with Charles Wallace?"

"The Echthroi are trying to destroy his mitochondria."

"But why would they bother with a child?"

"It is not always on the great or the important that the balance of the universe depends."

Louise the Larger whistled urgently, and Meg was almost sure that the snake was telling them that she would stay with Charles Wallace, that she would encourage him to keep on fighting to live. "Oh, Louise, please, please, you won't leave him? You *will* help him?"

"I will not leave him."

"Will he be all right?"

Louise answered with silence.

Blajeny said to Mr. Jenkins, "Charles Wallace will die if his mitochondria die. Do you understand that?"

Mr. Jenkins shook his head. "I thought he was making things up with his big words. I thought he was trying to show off. I didn't know there really were mitochondria."

Blajeny turned to Meg. "Explain."

"I'll try. But I'm not sure I really understand either, Mr. Jenkins. But I do know that we need energy to live. Okay?"

"Thus far."

She felt Blajeny kything information to her, and involuntarily her mind sorted it, simplified, put it into words which she hoped Mr. Jenkins would understand. "Well, each of our mitochondria has its own built-in system to limit the rate at which it burns fuel, okay, Mr. Jenkins?"

"Pray continue, Margaret."

"If the number of farandolae in any mitochondrion drops below a critical point, then hydrogen transport can't occur; there isn't enough fuel, and the result is death through energy lack." She felt the skin on her arms and legs prickling coldly. To put into words what might be happening within Charles Wallace was almost unendurable.

She felt Blajeny prodding her and continued. "Something's happening in Charles Wallace's mitochondria. I'm not sure what it is, because it's all words I don't know, but

his farandolae are dying—maybe they're killing each other
—no, that's not right. It sounds to me as though they're
refusing to sing, and that doesn't make any sense. The point
is that they're dying and so his mitochondria can't produce
enough oxygen." She broke off, angrily. "Blajeny! This is
all nonsense! How can we possibly stop them from doing
whatever it is they're doing, when they're so small they
aren't even visible? You've got to tell us! How can we help
Charles?"

Blajeny's kything was calm and cold as steel. "You will
know soon."

"Know what?"

"What you must do to overcome the Echthroi. When
you get there, my children, you will know."

"When we get where?"

"To one of Charles Wallace's mitochondria."

8 Journey into the Interior

Now that Blajeny had said it, it seemed to Meg the only logical, the only possible course of action. If they were to save Charles Wallace, if farandolae were causing his illness, if the Echthroi were at work within him as well as without, then the only hope was for them to become small enough to go into one of his mitochondria and see what was happening with the farandolae.

"Metron Ariston——" Calvin spoke softly. "Size. Where sizes don't matter. But——to be as small as a galaxy is huge: can you make us that small?"

Blajeny smiled. "Size is really quite relative."

"Anyhow"——Meg looked at Sporos——"we're already talking with a farandola." If she had tried to imagine a farandola, it would not have looked like Sporos.

Mr. Jenkins rose stiffly and moved with his peculiar stork-like gait to Blajeny. "I don't know why I thought I might be of help. This is all over my head. I will only be a hindrance to the children. You had better send me back to my school. At least there are no surprises for me there."

"What about this morning?" Blajeny asked. "That was not a surprise for you? I cannot tell you why you have been sent to us, Mr. Jenkins, because I myself do not yet know. But Meg Named you——"

"The full implications of this are not yet clear to me."

"It means that you are part of whatever is going to happen."

Mr. Jenkins moaned.

Blajeny stretched out his arms, embracing them all in the gesture. "The mitochondrion to which I am sending you is known as Yadah. It is Sporos's birthplace."

Sporos danced around, twingling in outrage.

Meg shouted at him, "If you are in Charles Wallace, if he's your galaxy, you couldn't be in a more special place!"

Louise sent her sibilant song towards Meg. All anger vanished when Meg caught, from Louise's song, another projection of Charles, huddled under the blankets. His mother lifted him to prop him up on pillows to ease his labored breathing, then pulled down the blankets so that Dr. Louise could listen to his heart with her stethoscope. She looked up gravely and Meg understood that she was suggesting that perhaps they had better call Brookhaven.

"Oxygen, then!" Meg cried out to Louise the Larger and Blajeny. "Wouldn't oxygen help Charles?"

"For a while. Dr. Colubra will see to that when the time comes."

Tears rushed to Meg's eyes. "Oh, Louise, take care of him. Don't let him stop fighting."

Mr. Jenkins asked, "Would anybody in his right mind let a snake near a sick child?"

"Dr. Louise will," Meg said, "I'm sure she will, from something she said in mother's lab the other night. Blajeny! Is Dr. Louise a Teacher, too?"

Blajeny nodded.

146

Meg's heart gave a leap of hope.

"Snakes," Mr. Jenkins murmured. "Mitochondria. Echthroi."

Meg swallowed a hiccupy sob, took off her glasses and wiped the tear-smeared lenses.

Mr. Jenkins looked at her and spoke in his most stilted, academic voice. "Man. The mean point in the universe. And Charles Wallace—is that it? At this moment in time Charles Wallace is the point of equilibrium?"

Blajeny nodded gravely.

"So what happens with his mitochondria and farandolae—?" He looked to Meg for explanation.

She tried to pull herself together. "Remember, Mr. Jenkins, you're great on Benjamin Franklin's saying, 'We must all hang together, or assuredly we will all hang separately.' That's how it is with human beings and mitochondria and farandolae—and our planet, too, I guess, and the solar system. We have to live together in—in harmony, or we won't live at all. So if something is wrong with Charles Wallace's mitochondria—" Her voice trailed off.

Mr. Jenkins shook his head. "What can we do? What can we possibly hope to do?" Then he cried out in horror. "Oh, no!"

The pseudo-Mr. Jenkins they had seen before was moving rapidly towards them. Louise reared her black coils upwards with a horrible hissing.

"Quickly!" Blajeny spread his arms wide, pulling Mr. Jenkins, Sporos, and Calvin into their span. Proginoskes caught Meg within the strength of his wings, the beat of

147

his heart. She seemed to become part of the cherubim's heartbeat.

The oval pupil dilated, and she went through to—

She could not tell where they were; she could only sense the presence of the others. As through a vast, echoing tunnel she heard Blajeny: "I would show you something to encourage you before you go."

Meg looked about. Ahead of her was a tremendous rhythmic swirl of wind and flame, but it was wind and flame quite different from the cherubim's; this was a dance, a dance ordered and graceful, and yet giving an impression of complete and utter freedom, of ineffable joy. As the dance progressed, the movement accelerated, and the pattern became clearer, closer, wind and fire moving together, and there was joy, and song, melody soaring, gathering together as wind and fire united.

And then wind, flame, dance, song, cohered in a great swirling, leaping, dancing, single sphere.

Meg heard Mr. Jenkins's incredulous, "What was *that?*"

Blajeny replied, "The birth of a star."

Mr. Jenkins protested, "But it's so small I could hold it in the palm of my hand." And then an indignant snort, "How big am I?"

"You must stop thinking about size, you know. It is both relative and irrelevant."

At this point Meg could not be bothered with size. She wanted to know something else. "Progo, will the star be Named?"

"He calls them all by name," the cherubim said.

148

Meg looked in wonder at the star. It was indeed so small that she could have reached out and caught it in her hand, but its flaming was so intense that the song itself came out of the fire and was part of the burning. She thought in wonder, —I must be the size of a galaxy.

And then all thoughts dissolved in the glory of the melody and the dance.

Blajeny's voice came like thunder, "Now!"

She was pulled into Proginoskes again, into the beat of the great heart, into the darkness of the eye, into the—

No!

She was being consumed by flame. She sensed a violent jolt to the cosmic rhythm, a distortion of wild disharmony—

She tried to scream, but no sound came. She felt pain so intense that she could not bear it another second; another second and the pain would annihilate her entirely.

Then the pain was gone, and she felt once again the rhythm of the cherubic heart, very rapid, faintly irregular. "Did it have to hurt that much?" Shock and pain made her loud and angry. Her limbs trembled weakly.

Proginoskes seemed to be having trouble; his heart continued to race unevenly. She thought she understood him to say, "We had a brush with an Echthros."

Her own breathing was a shallow panting. She felt that she was all there, all her atoms reassembled, that she was Meg; and yet when she opened her eyes she could see nothing but a strange, deep green-blackness. She listened, listened, and through what seemed at first to be a sound somewhat like the shrilling of insects on a summer night, she thought she could hear—or perhaps it was feel—a steady, regular pulsing.

"Progo, where are we?"

"Yadah."

"You mean we are *in* Charles Wallace? In one of his mitochondria?"

"Yes."

It was not conceivable. "What's that sort of thrumming I feel? Is it Charles Wallace's heartbeat?"

Proginoskes moved in negation in her mind. "It's the rhythm of Yadah."

"It feels like a heartbeat."

"Megling, we're not in earth time now; we're within Yadah. In farandolae time, Charles Wallace's heart beats something like once a decade."

She shivered. Her arms and legs still felt trembly and useless. She blinked, trying to adjust her eyes to the darkness. "Progo, I can't see."

"Nobody in the interior can see, Meg. Eyes aren't needed."

Her heart beat in frightened counterpoint to the rhythm of the mitochondrion. She could not pay proper attention as Proginoskes said, "It's what might be called a circadian rhythm. All life needs rhythm to—"

She interrupted. "Progo! Blajeny! I can't move!"

She felt Proginoskes within her thoughts. His own thinking had calmed considerably; he was recovering from whatever it was that had frightened him and caused her so much pain. "Blajeny did not come with us."

"Why?"

"This is no time for silly questions."

"Why is it silly? Why can't I see? Why can't I move?"

"Meg, you must stop panicking or I won't be able to kythe with you. We won't be able to help each other."

She made a tremendous effort to calm down, but with each heartbeat she felt only more tense, more frightened. How could her heart be pounding so rapidly if Charles Wallace's beat only once a decade?

Proginoskes thought noisily at her, "Time isn't any more important than size. All that is required of you is to be in the Now, in this moment which has been given us."

"I don't feel like myself. I'm *not* myself! I'm part of Charles Wallace."

"Meg. You are Named forever."

"But Progo—"

"Say the multiplication table."

"Now who's being silly?"

"Megling, it will help bring you to yourself. Try."

"I can't." Her mind felt battered and numb. She could not even remember enough to count to ten.

"What's 7 times 8?"

She responded automatically. "56."

"What's the product of 2/3 and 5/7."

Her mind whirled, cleared. "10 over 21."

"What's the next prime number after 67?"

"71."

"Can we think together now?" There was considerable concern in Proginoskes's questioning.

The concentration the cherubim had thrust on Meg had calmed her panic. "I'm okay. Where's Calvin? Where's Mr. Jenkins? And that—that Sporos?"

"They're all here. You'll be able to kythe with them soon. But first we have to find out what the second test is."

"Find out?" Her mind was still blurred from pain and fright.

He was patient with her. "As we found out what the first test was."

"You guessed that," she said. "Do you know what this one is?"

"I think it has to do with Sporos."

"But what?"

"This is what we must discover."

"We have to hurry, then." She tried to check her impatience.

"Meg, I have to work with you and Mr. Jenkins together, because he isn't capable of letting me move about in his mind as you can, so you'll have to help. The grown farandolae don't talk the way people do, they kythe."

"Like cherubim?"

"Some of the Ancient Ones, yes. With the younger ones it's a little closer to what you called mental telepathy. Never mind the degree; Mr. Jenkins can't understand kything at all, and you'll have to help him."

"I'll try. But you'll have to help me, Progo."

152

"Stretch out your right hand—"

"I can't move."

"That doesn't matter. Move your hand in your mind. Kythe it. Kythe that Mr. Jenkins is standing by you, and that you're reaching out to hold his hand. Are you doing it?"

"I'm trying."

"Can you feel his hand?"

"I think so. At least, I'm making believe I can."

"Hold it. Tightly. So that he knows you're there."

Her hand, which was no longer her hand in any way she had known before, nevertheless moved in the remembered pattern, and she thought she felt a slight pressure in return. She tried to kythe to the principal. "Mr. Jenkins, are you there?"

"Hheere." It was like an echo of a faintly remembered voice hoarse with chalk dust; but she knew that she and Mr. Jenkins were together.

"Meg, you will have to kythe him everything I tell you. If I move into his mind I hurt him; he can't absorb my energy. Now, try to translate simultaneously for him: make him see that a grown farandola's *matter* does not move, except as a plant does, or a tree when there is no breeze to cause its motion, or as the great kelp forests move. A grown farandola moves by kything. Kything is not going to be easy for Mr. Jenkins, because it has been a great many years since he's known himself, his real self."

Meg sighed with a kind of anxious fatigue, suddenly realizing the enormous amount of energy taken by this intense kything. The cherubim moved lightly, swiftly within

153

her, and his kything moved through and beyond her senses to an awareness she had never known before. She groped to contain it in images which were within Mr. Jenkins's comprehension.

The sea, a vast, curving, never-ending sea; it was as though they were in that sea, deep down under the water's surface, deeper than a whale can dive. The surface of the sea, and any light which might penetrate the surface, was hundreds of fathoms away. In the dark depths there was movement, movement which was part of the rhythm she had mistaken for Charles Wallace's heartbeat. The movement assumed shape and form, and images were kythed to her mind's eye, visual projections superimposed swiftly one over the other; she tried to send them to Mr. Jenkins:

a primordial fern forest;

a giant bed of kelp swaying to submarine currents;

a primeval forest of ancient trees with rough, silver bark;

underwater trees with silver-gold-green foliage which undulated regularly, rhythmically, not as though the long fronds were being blown by wind or current but of their own volition, like the undulation of those strange sea creatures halfway between plant life and animal life.

To the visual images music was added, strange, unearthly, rich, the surging song of the surrounding sea.

Farandolae.

She felt confusion and questioning from Mr. Jenkins. To him farandolae were little scampering creatures like Sporos, not like the sea trees she had been trying to show him.

154

Proginoskes kythed, "The sea trees, as you call them, are what Sporos will become when he Deepens. They are then called fara. Once he has Deepened he will no longer have to run about. A grown fara is far less limited than a human being is by time and place, because farae can be with each other any time in any place; distance doesn't separate them."

"They move without moving?" Meg asked.

"You might put it that way."

"Am I to learn to move without moving, too?"

"Yes, Meg. There's no other way in a mitochondrion. There's nothing for you to stand on in Yadah, and no space for you to move through. But because you're an earthling, and earthlings excel in adaptability, you can learn this motionless motion. Are you translating for Mr. Jenkins?"

"I'm trying."

"Keep on, Meg. We'll have time to rest later, unless—" She felt a small, sharp pain, which was immediately withdrawn. "Some of the Ancient Ones can kythe not only from mitochondrion to mitochondrion within their human hosts, but to farandolae on mitochondria in other human hosts. Do you remember how shocked Sporos was when Calvin told him that human beings can't do that kind of thing?"

"Yes, but Progo, Mr. Jenkins doesn't understand about Sporos running around like a toy mouse. I don't understand it either. He isn't a bit like the sort of sea things you just showed us."

"Sporos is, as he said, only a child, although he was juggling chronologies when he said he was born yesterday. A

155

farandola well into adolescence has already passed through its early stages and taken root and is becoming a grown fara. It is nearly time for Sporos to leave childhood and Deepen. If he does not, it will be another victory for the Echthroi."

"But why wouldn't he Deepen?"

"Calvin is having trouble kything with him. Sporos is holding back. We have to help him Deepen, Meg. That's our second test, I'm sure it is."

To make an unwilling Sporos Deepen; it seemed a more impossible ordeal than Naming one of three Mr. Jenkinses. "How do we do it?"

He countered with another question. "Are you calm?"

Calm! Then, once again, she moved into that strange place which is on the other side of feeling. With one part of herself she knew that she was in Charles Wallace, actually inside her brother; that she was so small that she couldn't be seen in the most powerful micro-electron microscope, or heard in the micro-sonarscope; she knew, too, that Charles Wallace's life depended on what was going to happen now. She was beginning to get a glimmer of what Proginoskes meant when he talked about the dangers of feeling. She held herself very still, very cold, then turned towards the cherubim in quiet kything.

"Be a fara," he told her. "Make believe. Do the inhabitants of Yadah seem more limited than human beings because once they have taken root they can't move from their Deepening Place? But human beings need Deepening Places, too. And far too many never have any. Think about

156

your Deepening Places, Meg. Open yourself into kything. Open."

She returned to the strange world which was below light, below sound, penetrated only by the rhythm of tides pulled by the moon, by the sun, by the rhythm of the earth itself. She became one with the kything, Deepened creatures moving in the intricate pattern of song, of the loveliness of rhythm, of joy.

Then a coldness came, a horrible, blood-freezing chill. Tendrils were drawn back, pulled away from her, isolating themselves, isolating Meg, Proginoskes, each other. The song jerked, out of rhythm, out of tune, rejecting her—

Something was wrong, horrifyingly wrong—

She felt Proginoskes hurling himself at her, into her. "Meg! That's enough for now. We must be with the others, Calvin, Mr. Jenkins, Sporos, before—"

"Before what?"

"Before the second test. We must all be together. Open. Kythe to Calvin."

"Where is he?"

"It doesn't matter where he is, Meg. You've got to get it through your head that *where* doesn't make any difference in a mitochondrion. It's why. And how. And who."

"Calvin—" She seemed to feel every muscle in her body straining, and protesting at the strain.

"You're trying too hard," the cherubim said. "Relax, Megling. You kythe with me without all that effort. You and Calvin often kythe without realizing it. And when Charles Wallace knows when something's upset you at

157

school, knows it even before you come home, that's kything. Just be Meg. Open. Be. Kythe."

Through the darkness of under-sea she kythed. "Calvin—"

"Meg!"

"Where are you?"

Proginoskes flicked sharply at her. "Forget where."

"How are you?"

"All right. A little confused by everything. Sporos—"

"Where—no, *how* is Sporos?"

"Meg, he doesn't want to kythe or be with me. He doesn't want to share his world. He says that human beings are unworthy, and that may be so, but—"

She felt a swirling of kything all around her, as though the words and images of the kything were the drops of water which go to make up the ocean, drops of water which are not separate one from the other as human beings are separate. Within the flowing of the deep tides images flashed by, many little creatures like Sporos, scampering about, carefree, merry, always in the protection of the great kelp-fern-trees, the Deepened Ones, about which they flitted and fluttered.

"Are you translating for Mr. Jenkins?"

"I'm trying, Progo, but I'm not sure I really feel him. I know that I'm with you, and with Calvin, but Mr. Jenkins—"

"Be with him, Meg. He needs you. He's frightened."

"If Blajeny wanted him along, there must be a reason for it. But it seems to me he's an awful liability."

She thought she felt a thin, distant "I am aware of that."

She stretched herself towards that faint response. "Mr. Jenkins—"

"That's right," Proginoskes said. "Remember, he hasn't much imagination. Or, rather, it's been frozen for a long while and hasn't had time to thaw. You'll have to kythe your whole self to him; you'll have to hold his hand, tightly, so that he can feel you and return your kythe. Can you feel his hand?"

"I—I imagine so."

"Can he feel you?"

"Mr. Jenkins! Mr. Jenkins?" she kythed questioningly. "Wait a minute, Progo, Cal, I'm not sure, something's wrong—" She broke off, gasped, "Calvin! Progo! Pro—" With every particle of herself she screamed, not a scream made with her voice, but with all of her, a scream of pain that was beyond terror.

It was the same pain that had torn across a galaxy when Proginoskes had shown her the Xing of the Echthroi; it was the pain which had slashed across the sky in the schoolyard when she had Named Mr. Jenkins; it was the pain which had almost annihilated her when Proginoskes took her the strange journey through his eye to Yadah.

She was being Xed.

9 Farandolae and Mitochondria

This was the end of Meg. There was to be no more anything. Ever. Exit Meg. Ex-Meg. X-Meg.

Then she realized that if she could think this, if she could think at all, then it was not happening. One who is Xed cannot think. The pain still burned like ice, but she could think through it. She still was.

With all of her she kythed away from the Xness. "Progo! Calvin! Help me!"

Through her cries she felt the cherubim. "Meg! I Name you! You are!"

And then numbers, numbers moving as strong and steady and rhythmic as tide.

Calvin. He was sending numbers to her, Calvin was sending back to her those first trigonometry problems they had done together. She held on to the strength of numbers as to a lifeline, until the Echthroi-pain was gone and she was free to move back into the realm of words again, human words which were much easier for Calvin than numbers.

"Calvin," she called. "Oh, Calvin." And then her kything was an anguished longing for her parents. Where was her father? Had Dr. Louise or her mother called Brookhaven? What had they told her father? Was he on his way home? And her mother—she wanted to retreat, reverse, revert, to climb back into her mother's lap as she had done when she was Charles Wallace's age and needed healing from some small hurt . . .

No, Meg.

She felt as though gentle fingers were pushing her down, forcing her to walk alone. She tried to kythe, to get her mind's voice into focus, sent its beam at last to Proginoskes and Calvin. "What happened?"

She felt a series of major earthquakes before Proginoskes managed words for her. Whatever it was that had happened, it had certainly upset the cherubim. He kythed at last, "As though once weren't enough, when you reached out for Mr. Jenkins's hand you got an Echthros-Mr. Jenkins. Now we know that at least one of them followed us here."

"How?"

"Not through Mr. Jenkins, though it's still using a Jenkins-body. Perhaps Sporos—"

"Sporos!"

"Pride has always been the downfall of the Deepening Ones. Sporos may have listened to an Echthros—we aren't sure."

"What did you do? How did you get me away from it? It hurt—it hurt more than I knew anything could hurt. And then I felt you Naming me, Progo, and you, Cal, you were sending numbers to me, and the pain went and I was back into myself again."

Calvin kythed, "Proginoskes got a lot of little farandolae to rush up and tickle the Echthros-Mr. Jenkins. It was so startled, it let you go."

"Where is it now—the Echthros-Mr. Jenkins?"

Proginoskes was sharp. "It doesn't matter where, Meg. It's here. It's with us in Yadah."

"Then we're still in danger from it?"

"All Yadah is in danger. Every mitochondrion in this human host is in danger."

"This human host?"

Proginoskes did not reply. This human host was Charles Wallace.

"What are we going to do?"

There was another volcanic upheaval before Proginoskes replied, "We must not give way to panic."

She kythed Calvinwards and felt him returning the kything. She asked, "Did you know what was happening to me?"

"Not at first. Then Progo told me." There was a terrible quietness to Calvin's reply. She felt that he was holding something back from her.

"The little farandolae—the ones who saved me—are they all right?"

There was silence.

"Are they all right, the little farandolae who startled the Echthros and saved me?"

"No." The kything came reluctantly from both Calvin and Proginoskes.

"What happened to them?"

"To surprise an Echthros is not a safe thing to do."

"The Echthros Xed them?"

"No, Meg. They Xed themselves. That's a very different matter."

"What will happen to them now?"

Proginoskes kythed slowly, "I've never seen it happen before. I've heard about it, but I've never seen it. Now I understand more than I used to. The farandolae are known by name just as the stars are. That's all I need to know."

"You haven't told me anything! Where are the little farandolae who saved me? If they Xed themselves, then where are they?"

She heard a faint "Where doesn't matter. Meg, you must get in touch with Mr. Jenkins. The real Mr. Jenkins."

Instinctively she withdrew her kything. "I don't dare try again. Do you have any idea how much that hurt?"

"Your scream shook the entire mitochondrion. I only hope it didn't hurt Charles Wallace."

She flinched, then held on to something, she wasn't sure what, but it felt like a lifeline. After a moment she knew that it was coming from the cherubim, an outflowing of love, love so tangible that she could hold on to it.

"Reach for Mr. Jenkins," Proginoskes urged. "Name him for himself again. See how much you've been able to kythe to him. And remember, you have to go at his speed, not your own."

"Why! He's holding us back!"

"Hush, Meg." Calvin kythed. "Adults take longer at this kind of thing than we do, particularly adults like Mr. Jenkins who hasn't tried new thoughts for a long time."

"But we don't have time! Charles Wallace—"

"I said he takes longer than we do, and that's true. But sometimes adults can go deeper than we can, if we're patient."

163

"We don't have time to be patient!"

"Meg, trust Blajeny. Mr. Jenkins must be with us for a reason. Help him. Do what Progo says."

Proginoskes kythed urgently, "We may need Mr. Jenkins to get Sporos to Deepen. Blajeny wouldn't have sent him unless—oh, Meg, a Teacher never does anything without reason. Try to reach Mr. Jenkins, Meg."

She pushed her terror aside and opened herself to kything and she was with Charles Wallace,
not within him,
not without him,
but with him,
part of his exhaustion,
his terrifying energy loss,
his struggle to breathe.

Oh, fight, Charles,
don't stop struggling,
breathe,
breathe,
I'll try to help,
I'll do anything I can to help, even

then

She was with the twins. Charles Wallace, she thought, had sent her.

The twins were in the garden, digging, grimly spading up and turning under the old tomato plants, the frost-blackened zinnias, the lettuce gone to seed, turning them

under to enrich the earth for the next spring, the next plant-
ing, with set faces working silently, taking out their anxiety over Charles Wallace in physical labor.

Sandy broke the silence. "Where's Meg?"

Dennys paused, his foot on his pitchfork as he pressed
it into the earth. "She should be getting home from school
soon."

"Charles Wallace said she isn't in school. He said that
Meg is *in* him. I heard him."

"Charles Wallace is delirious."

"Have you ever seen anyone die?"

"Only animals."

"I wish Meg would come home."

"So do I."

They went on with their preparation of the garden for
the winter cold and snow.

—If the twins' job is simply to take care of their garden
—Meg told herself, —your job is to reach Mr. Jenkins.
Where? Nowhere. Just Mr. Jenkins.

"Mr. Jenkins. Mr. Jenkins. You are you and nobody
else and I Named you. I'm kything, Mr. Jenkins. Here I
am. Me. Meg. You know me and I know you."

She thought she heard a sniff, a Mr. Jenkins sniff. Then
he seemed to recede again. This minuscule undersea world
was totally beyond his comprehension. She tried to kythe
to him once more all the images in earth equivalents which
she had received, but he responded with nothing beyond
anxious blankness.

"Name him," Proginoskes urged. "He is afraid to be.

When you Named him in the schoolyard, that was kything, that was how you knew him from the two Echthroi-Mr. Jenkinses, how you must know him this time."

Mr. Jenkins. Unique, as every star in the sky is unique, every leaf on every tree, every snowflake, every farandola, every cherubim, unique: Named.

He gave Calvin shoes. And he didn't have to come with us to this danger and horribleness, but he did. He chose to throw in his lot with us when he could have gone back to school and his safe life as a failure.

Yes, but for an unimaginative man to come with them into the unimaginably infinitesimal unknown isn't the kind of thing a failure does.

Nevertheless, Mr. Jenkins had done it, was doing it.

"Mr. Jenkins, I love you!"

She did.

Without stopping to think she put her imagined hand into his. His fingers were slightly damp and chill, just as clammy as she had always thought Mr. Jenkins's hand would be.

And real.

10 Yadah

Of course Mr. Jenkins's hand would be damp. He'd be scared out of his wits. He was years away from games of Make Believe and Let's Pretend.

"Mr. Jenkins, are you all right?"

She felt a fumbling kything, a frightened inability to accept that they were actually in a mitochondrion, a mitochondrion within one of Charles Wallace's cells. "How long have we been here?"

"I'm not sure. So much has happened. Progo—you're sure we're in farandola time, not earth time?"

"Farandola time."

"Whew!" she told Mr. Jenkins in relief. "That means that time on earth is passing much more slowly than time is for us—aeons more slowly. Charles Wallace's heart beats only once every decade or so."

"Even so," Proginoskes warned, "there's no time to waste."

Another flash of Charles Wallace's face, ashen, eyes closed, breathing labored; of her mother's face, tight with pain; of Dr. Louise, watchful, waiting. She stood with her small hand lightly against Charles Wallace's wrist.

"I know," Meg answered the cherubim. A cold wind seemed to blow through the interstices of her ribs. She must be strong for Charles Wallace now, so that he could draw on that strength. She held her mind quiet and steady until it calmed.

Then she opened herself again to Mr. Jenkins. Muddied thoughts which could hardly qualify as kything moved about her like sluggish water, and yet she understood that Mr. Jenkins was being more open with her than he had ever been before, or than he ever was able to be with most people. His mind shuddered into Meg's as he tried to grasp the extraordinary fact that he was still himself, still Mr. Jenkins, at the same time that he was a minuscule part of the child who had been one of his most baffling and irritating problems at school.

Meg tried to let him know, in as unalarming a way as possible, that at least one of the Echthroid-Mr. Jenkinses was with them on Yadah. She did not want to recall her terror during her encounter with one of them, but she had to help Mr. Jenkins understand.

He sent her a response, first of bafflement, then fear, then a strange tenderness towards her. "You should not be asked to endure such things, Margaret."

"There's more," she told him. This more was hardest of all, to make him understand that some of the little farandolae, some of the playful, dancing creatures, had saved her from the Echthros-Mr. Jenkins, and had sacrificed themselves in doing so.

Mr. Jenkins groaned.

From Proginoskes Meg relayed to the principal, "It was better than letting the Echthroi X them. They're still—they're still part of Creation this way." She turned her kything to Proginoskes. "If the Echthroi X something, or if something Xs itself, is it forever?"

The cherubim surrounded her with the darkness of his unknowing. "But we don't need to know, Meg," he told her firmly, and the darkness began to blow away. "I am a cherubim. All I need to know is that all the galaxies, all the stars, all creatures, cherubic, human, farandolan, all, all, are known by Name." He seemed almost to be crooning to himself.

Meg kythed at him sharply. "You're Progo. I'm Meg. He's Mr. Jenkins. Now what are we supposed to do?"

Proginoskes came back into focus. "Mr. Jenkins does not want to understand what a farandola is."

"Evil is evil," Mr. Jenkins sent fumblingly Megwards. She felt his mind balking at the idea of communication where distance was no barrier. "Mice talk by squeaking, and shrimp by—I don't know much marine biology, but they must make *some* sound. But trees!" he expostulated. "Mice who put down roots and turn into trees—you did say trees?"

"No." Meg was impatient, not so much at Mr. Jenkins as at her own ineptitude in communicating with him. "The farae—well, they aren't unlike trees, sort of primordial ones, and they aren't unlike coral and underwater things like that."

"Trees cannot talk with each other."

"Farae can. And as for trees—don't they?"

"Nonsense."

"Mr. Jenkins, when you walk through the woods at

169

home, and the wind moves in the trees, don't you ever have the feeling that if you knew how, you'd be able to understand what they were saying?"

"Never." It had been a long time since he had walked in the woods. He moved from his lodgings to the school, from the school to his lodgings, driving himself both ways. He did not have time to go for walks in the woods . . .

She felt a dim regret in his kything, so she tried to make him hear the sound of wind in the pine woods. "If you close your eyes it sounds like ocean waves, even though we're not anywhere near the ocean."

All she felt from Mr. Jenkins was another cold wash of incomprehension.

So she envisioned a small grove of aspens for him, each leaf shivering and shaking separately, whispering softly in the still summer air.

"I'm too old," was Mr. Jenkins's response. "I'm much too old. I'm just holding you back. You ought to return me to Earth."

Meg forgot that she had recently made exactly that suggestion. "Anyhow, Yadah is on Earth, or in Earth, sort of, since it's in Charles Wallace . . ."

"No, no," Mr. Jenkins said, "it's too much. I'm no help. I don't know why I thought I might be—" His kything trailed off.

Through his discouragement she became aware of Calvin. "Hey, Meg! Communication implies sound. Communion doesn't." He sent her a brief image of walking

170

silently through the woods, the two of them alone together, their feet almost noiseless on the rusty carpet of pine needles. They walked without speaking, without touching, and yet they were as close as it is possible for two human beings to be. They climbed up through the woods, coming out into the brilliant sunlight at the top of the hill. A few sumac trees showed their rusty candles. Mountain laurel, shiny, so dark a green the leaves seemed black in the fierceness of sunlight, pressed towards the woods. Meg and Calvin had stretched out in the thick, late-summer grass, lying on their backs and gazing up into the shimmering blue of sky, a vault interrupted only by a few small clouds.

And she had been as happy, she remembered, as it is possible to be, and as close to Calvin as she had ever been to anybody in her life, even Charles Wallace, so close that their separate bodies, daisies and buttercups joining rather than dividing them, seemed a single enjoyment of summer and sun and each other.

That was surely the purest kind of kything.

Mr. Jenkins had never had that kind of communion with another human being, a communion so rich and full that silence speaks more powerfully than words.

Again Calvin was kything with quick, urgent words. *"The Wall Street Journal."*

"What!"

"Mr. Jenkins reads *The Wall Street Journal*. Maybe he might have read this."

"Read what?"

171

"You remember, just a few weeks ago I was telling you about a science project I did years ago when I was in fourth grade. Even the twins were interested."

Meg listened intently, trying to kythe simultaneously to Mr. Jenkins.

The subject of the old science project had come up because of the twins' garden. Sandy and Dennys were baffled and irritated. Some of the pepper plants had large, firm, healthy fruit. On others the peppers were wizened and wrinkled and pale. Calvin had been taken out to look at the undersized, flabby plants, which showed no visible sign of disease, and he had been reminded of his fourth-grade science project.

Meg asked, "Could the plants be having the same kind of trouble mitochondria are having? Could Echthroi bother things like gardens?"

Calvin pushed this question aside to think about later. "Not now, Meg. Listen. I think my science project will help Mr. Jenkins understand."

Meg seemed to see Mr. Jenkins's nose twitching as it always did when he was reluctant.

"Okay, then." She kythed to him, slowly, as simply as possible, Calvin's kything always a strong current under and through hers.

At nine years of age Calvin read avidly, every book that came into the small village library. The librarian, seeing his pleasure in books, encouraged him, gave him a special corner in the library as his own, and gave him all the old classics of the imagination to read. His span of concentration on these stories was infinite.

But he considered most of the work he was given at school a bore, particularly science projects. However, he was also fiercely competitive, and determined to be the top of his class in all subjects, even those he considered a waste of time.

When the week came when he must turn in the topic for his science project by Friday, he was disinterested and planless, but he knew he had to choose something. He was thinking about this with particular urgency on Thursday afternoon when he was helping old Mrs. Buncombe clean out her attic. What could he choose which would interest the teacher and class and not bore him completely? Mrs. Buncome was not paying him for the dirty and dusty job—her attic had not been touched for years—but she had bribed him to do it by telling him that there was an old set of china up in the attic, and he could take it as payment. Perhaps she knew that the O'Keefes could never sit down to a meal together, even if they had wanted to, because there weren't enough plates and cups and saucers to go round.

The china was in a box at the back of the attic, and it was wrapped in old newspapers. Some of it was broken; much of it was cracked; it certainly was not a set of forgotten Wedgwood or Dresden. Who had bothered to wrap it up as carefully as though it were a priceless heirloom? However, there was enough of the set left to make it worth taking home. He unwrapped it for his mother, who complained ungraciously, if correctly, that it was junk.

He cleared up the crumpled, yellowed newspapers, and began to read one. It was an old *Wall Street Journal;* the date had been torn off, but the paper was brittle and stained and he knew that it must be a good many years old. His eye caught an article about a series of experiments made by a biologist.

The biologist had the idea, unusual at the time, that plants were capable of subjective reactions to stimuli, and he decided to measure the strength of these reactions by attaching electrodes, like those used in a lie detector, to the leaves of a large, healthy philodendron.

At that point in the account a section of paper was torn away, and Calvin lost several sentences. He picked up a statement that electronic needles would record the plant's responses on a graph, much as brain waves or heart patterns are recorded by the electro-encephalogram or electrocardiogram machines.

The biologist spent an entire morning looking at the needles moving in a straight line across the paper. Nothing happened. No reactions. The needle did not quiver. The line moved slowly and steadily.

The biologist thought, "I'll make that plant react. I'll burn one of its leaves."

The stylus made wild up and down markings of alarm.

The rest of the article was torn off.

Mr. Jenkins's thoughts came to Meg quite clearly, a little

174

irritably. "I read that article. I thought it was nonsense. Just some crackpot."

Calvin kythed, "Most major scientific discoveries have been made by crackpots—or at least, people who were thought to be crackpots."

"My own parents, for instance," Meg added, "until some of their discoveries were proved to be true."

Calvin continued. "Listen. There's more. I found another article among the papers."

This one described the biologist going on a cross-country lecturing tour. He asked one of his students to take care of, watch, and record the reactions of his philodendron.

The plant's alarm needles jumped nervously whenever the biologist's plane took off or landed.

"How would it know?" Meg asked.

"It did."

"But distance," she protested, "how could a plant, just an ordinary domestic philodendron, know what was happening miles and miles away?"

"Or care," came dourly from Mr. Jenkins.

"Distance doesn't seem to be any more important than size. Or time. As for caring—well, that's outside the realm of provable fact."

For his project Calvin had worked out a variation on the theme of plant response. He had no way of measuring the subjective responses of a plant, so he decided to plant three bean seeds.

Mr. Jenkins did not think much of this.

Meg kythed him a warning, "Wait! This was all Calvin's

175

own idea. He was only nine years old then, and he didn't know that experiments of the same kind were already being made."

Calvin planted one of the seeds in a pot which he left in the kitchen at home. He put it on a windowsill where it would get sunlight, and he watered it daily. His brothers and sisters were warned that if they touched it they'd get clobbered. They knew he meant it, and they left his plant physically alone. However, the plant heard—

"Without ears?" Mr. Jenkins kythed crossly.

"Like Louise, maybe," Meg returned.

The plant heard the automatic ugly invective of daily speech in Calvin's home. Calvin himself stayed in the house as little as possible.

The other two seeds he took to the library, where the librarian gave him permission to put his pots in two sunny windows. One of these beans he watered and cared for dutifully. That was all. The third bean he talked to, encouraging it, urging it to grow. When the first green shoot appeared he lavished on it all the love which had so little outlet in his home. He sat, after school, close by his plant, doing his homework, reading aloud when nobody was around, sharing.

The first of the bean plants, the one in the O'Keefe's kitchen, was puny, and too pale a green, like the twins' sickly peppers. The second plant, in the library window, the plant given regular care but no special time or attention, grew normally. The third plant, the plant Calvin loved, grew strong and green and unusually large and healthy.

Mr. Jenkins kythed thinly but quite comprehensibly, "If

176

philodendron and beans can react like that, it should help me to understand farandolae—is that what you're trying to tell me?"

"Sort of," Meg replied.

Calvin added, "See? Distance doesn't matter. They can know and converse with each other and distance doesn't really exist for them."

Mr. Jenkins sent out waves of disbelief. "And if they're loved, they'll grow? And if they aren't loved—"

"The Echthroi can move in."

Now she heard what could only be Sporos's twingling. "They're dull and slow, like all human beings, but you're getting through to them at last, cherub."

"My name is Proginoskes, if you please, mouse-creature."

The farandola was not amused. "My name is Sporos." A reproving twingle.

"Meg." Proginoskes kythed deeply into her. "Do you realize what has just been happening? You've been close to Mr. Jenkins, haven't you?"

"I guess so. Yes."

"And yet your bodies are not close together. And you already know that nothing can separate you from Calvin when you kythe together."

Yes. She was with Calvin. They were together. She felt the warmth of his quick smile, a smile which always had a slight quirk of sadness and acceptance unusual in a sixteen-year-old. He was not kything in words now, but in great waves of courage, of strength, flowing over and through her.

She accepted it, absorbed it. Fortitude. She was going

to need a great deal. She opened herself, drank it in.

"All right," Proginoskes told them. "We are together. We can continue."

"What are we to do?" Mr. Jenkins asked.

"The second test," the cherubim urged. "We must pass the second test."

"And that is?"

"To Name Sporos. As Meg had to Name you."

"But Sporos is already Named!"

"Not until he has Deepened."

"I don't understand."

"When Sporos Deepens," Proginoskes told Mr. Jenkins, "it means that he comes of age. It means that he grows up. The temptation for farandola or for man or for star is to stay an immature pleasure-seeker. When we seek our own pleasure as the ultimate good we place ourselves as the center of the universe. A fara or a man or a star has his place in the universe, but nothing created is the center."

Meg asked, "The little farandolae who saved me—"

"They came of age, Meg."

She pondered this. "I *think* I understand—"

"I don't," Mr. Jenkins said. "I thought we came here to try to help Charles Wallace, that he is ill because of his mitochondria—"

Proginoskes pushed back impatience. "He is."

"But what does Sporos have to do with Charles Wallace?"

"The balance of life within Yadah is precarious. If Sporos and the others of his generation do not Deepen, the balance will be altered. If the farandolae refuse to Deepen, the song

178

will be stilled, and Charles Wallace will die. The Echthroi will have won."

"But a child—" Mr. Jenkins asked. "One small child—why is he so important?"

"It is the pattern throughout Creation. One child, one man, can swing the balance of the universe. In your own Earth history what would have happened if Charlemagne had fallen at Roncesvalles? One minor skirmish?"

"It would have been an Echthroi victory?"

"And your history would have been even darker than it is."

"Mr. Jenkins!" Meg called. "Listen, I just remembered: For want of a nail the shoe was lost; for want of a shoe the horse was lost; for want of a horse the rider was lost; for want of a rider the message was lost; for want of the message the battle was lost; for want of the battle the war was lost; for want of the war the kingdom was lost; and all for the want of a horseshoe nail."

"We must save Charles Wallace!" Mr. Jenkins cried. "What can we do, Progo? What can we do?"

11 Sporos

A burst of harmony so brilliant that it almost overwhelmed them surrounded Meg, the cherubim, Calvin, and Mr. Jenkins. But after a moment of breathlessness, Meg was able to open herself to the song of the farae, these strange creatures who were Deepened, rooted, yet never separated from each other, no matter how great the distance.

We are the song of the universe. We sing with the angelic host. We are the musicians. The farae and the stars are the singers. Our song orders the rhythm of creation.

Calvin asked, "How can you sing with the *stars?*"

There was surprise at the question: it is the song. We sing it together. That is our joy. And our Being.

"But how do you know about stars—in here—inside—"

How could farae not know about stars when farae and stars sing together?

"You can't see the stars. How can you possibly know about them?"

Total incomprehension from the farae. If Meg and Calvin kythed in visual images, this was their limitation. The farae had moved beyond physical sight.

"Okay," Calvin said. "I know how little of ourselves, and of our brains, we've learned to use. We have billions of brain cells, and we use only the tiniest portion of them."

Mr. Jenkins added with his dry, ropy kythe, "I have heard that the number of cells in the brain and the number of stars in the universe is said to be exactly equal."

"Progo!" Meg asked. "You memorized the names of all the stars—how many are there?"

"How many? Great heavens, earthling, I haven't the faintest idea."

"But you said your last assignment was to memorize the names of all of them."

"I did. All the stars in all the galaxies. And that's a great many."

"But how many?"

"What difference does it make? I know their *names*. I don't know how many there are. It's their names that matter."

The strong kything of the farae joined Proginoskes. "And the song. If it were not for the support of the singing of the galaxies, we farae on Yadah would have lost the melody, so few of the farandolae are Deepening. The un-Namers are at work."

Meg felt a sudden chill, a pulling back, a fading of the Deepened farae; there was dissonance in the harmony; the rhythm faltered.

In her mind's eye an image was flashed of a troop of farandolae dancing wildly about one fara-tree, going faster and faster, until she felt dizzy.

"Sporos is with them," Proginoskes told her.

"What are they doing? Why are they spinning faster and faster?" The circle of farandolae revolved so rapidly that it became a swirling blur. The fronds of the great fara around whom they swirled began to droop.

"They are absorbing the nourishment which the fara needs. The fara is Senex, from whom Sporos came." There was chill in Proginoskes's words.

The speed of the dancing farandolae became like a scream in Meg's ears. "Stop!" she cried. "Stop it at once!" There was nothing merry or joyful in the dance. It was savage, wild, furious.

Then, through the raging of the dance came a strong, pure strain of melody, quiet, certain, noble. The dancing farandolae broke their circle and scampered about aimlessly; then, led by Sporos, they raced to another fara and began circling it.

The fronds of Senex greened, lifted.

Proginoskes said, "He is strong enough to hold out longer than any of the other farae. But even Senex cannot hold out forever." He stopped abruptly. "Feel."

"Feel?"

"The rhythm of the mitochondrion. Is it my fearfulness, or is Yadah faltering?"

"It is not you," Meg answered the cherubim. They were all very still, listening, feeling. Again there came a slight irregularity in the steady pulsing. A faltering. A missed beat. Then it steadied, continued.

Like a gash through the non-light of Yadah Meg had a brief vision of Charles Wallace lying in his small room, gasping for air. She thought she saw Dr. Louise, but the strange thing was that she could not tell whether it was Dr.

Louise Colubra, or Louise the actual colubra. "Don't give up. Breathe, Charles. Breathe." And a steady voice, "It's time to try oxygen."

Then she was drawn back within the mitochondrion to Senex, the parent tree of Sporos. She tried to convey to him what she had just seen, but she received nothing from him in return. His incomprehension was even greater than Mr. Jenkins's had been. She asked Proginoskes, "Does Senex know that Charles Wallace even exists?"

"As you know that your galaxy, the Milky Way, exists."

"Does he know that Charles Wallace is ill?"

"As you know that your Earth is ill, by fish dying in the rivers, birds dying in the forests, people dying in the choked cities. You know by war and hate and chaos. Senex knows his mitochondrion is ill because the farandolae will not Deepen and many farae are dying. Listen. Kythe."

A group of farandolae whirled about a fara; fronds drooped; color drained. The dance was a scream of laughter, ugly laughter. Meg smelled the stench which was like the stench in the twins' garden when she had first encountered an Echthros.

She heard a voice. It was like a bad tape recording of Mr. Jenkins. "You need not Deepen and lose your power to move, to dance. No one can force you to. Do not listen to the farae. Listen to me."

The great central trunk of the surrounded fara began to weaken.

Meg tried to project herself into the dance, to break the vortex. "Sporos, come out! Don't listen. You were sent

183

to the Teacher. You belong with us. Come out, Sporos, you are meant to Deepen!"

Then it was as though she were the end skater in a violent game of crack-the-whip and suddenly was flung so wildly across the ice that she crashed into the end of the rink. The force with which she had been thrown was so fierce that her kything was completely blacked out.

"Breathe, Meg, breathe." It was Proginoskes, using the same words which Louise was using with Charles Wallace. "Breathe, Meg. You're all right."

She reeled, staggered, regained her balance.

Again she heard the ugly laugh, and the false Mr. Jenkins voice urging, "Kill the fara!"

Then came Mr. Jenkins's own voice. "I see. I understand." She felt emanating from him a dry, dusty acknowledgment of unpleasant fact.

She returned sharply, still slightly breathless, *"I* don't understand."

Mr. Jenkins asked her, "Why did Hitler want to control the world? Or Napoleon? Or Tiberius?"

"I don't know. I don't know why anyone would. I think it would be awful."

"But you admit that they did, Margaret?"

"They wanted to," she conceded. "But they didn't succeed."

"They did a remarkably good job of succeeding for a period of time, and they will not lightly be forgotten. A great many people perished during the years of their rules."

184

"But farandolae—why would little farandolae like Sporos—"

"They appear to be not that unlike human beings."

She felt cold and quiet. Once Mr. Jenkins had accepted the situation, he understood it better than she did. She asked, "Okay, then, what have the Echthroi got to do with it? They're behind it, aren't they?"

Proginoskes answered, "The Echthroi are always behind war."

Meg turned in anguish towards Senex, calm and strong as an oak tree, but, unlike the oak, pliable, able to bend with wind and weather. "Senex, we've been sent to help, but I'm not strong enough to fight the Echthroi. I can't stop Sporos and the other farandolae from killing the fara. Oh, Senex, if they succeed, won't they kill themselves, too?"

Senex responded coldly, quietly. "Yes."

"This is insane," Mr. Jenkins said.

Proginoskes answered, "All war is insane."

"But, as I understand it," Mr. Jenkins continued, "we are a minutely immeasurable part of Charles Wallace?"

"We are."

"Therefore if, while we are on—or, rather, in—this mito-chondrion, if Charles Wallace were to die, then—er—um— we—"

"Die, too."

"Then I fight not only for Charles Wallace's life but for Meg's, and Calvin's, and—"

"Your own."

Meg felt Mr. Jenkins's total indifference to his own life. She was not yet willing to accept the burden of his concern for her. "We musn't think about that! We musn't think about anything but Charles!"

Proginoskes wound around and through her thoughts: "You cannot show your concern for Charles Wallace now except in concern for Sporos. Don't you understand that we're all part of one another, and the Echthroi are trying to splinter us, in just the same way that they're trying to destroy all Creation?"

The dancing farandolae whirled and screamed, and Meg thought she could hear Sporos's voice: "We're not part of anybody! We're farandolae, and we're going to take over Yadah. After that—"

A hideous screech of laughter assailed Meg's ears. Again she flung herself at the dance, trying to pull Sporos out of it.

Senex drew her back with the power of his kythe. "Not that way, not by force."

"But Sporos has to Deepen! He has to!"

Then, around the edges of her awareness, Meg heard a twingling, and Calvin was with Sporos, trying to reach out to him, to kythe with him.

Sporos's response was jangly, but he came out of the wild circle and hovered on its periphery. "Why did Blajeny send you alien life forms to Yadah with me? How can you possibly help with my schooling? We make music by ourselves. We don't need you."

Meg felt Proginoskes's volcanic upheaving, felt a violent wind, searing tongues of flame. "Idiot, idiot," Progi-

186

noskes was sending, "we all need each other. Every atom in the universe is dependent on every other."

"I don't need you."

Suddenly Proginoskes kythed quietly and simply, "I need you, Sporos. We all of us need you. Charles Wallace needs you."

"I don't need Charles Wallace."

Calvin kythed urgently, "Don't you? What happens to you if something happens to Charles Wallace? Who have you been listening to?"

Sporos withdrew. Meg could not feel him at all.

Calvin emanated frustration. "I can't reach him. He slips away from me every time I think I'm getting close."

Sporos was pulled back into the whirling circle. The surrounded fara was limp, all life draining rapidly. Senex mourned, "His song is going out."

Proginoskes kythed, "Xed. Snuffed out like a candle."

Senex's fronds drooped in grief. "Sporos and his generation listen to those who would silence the singing. They listen to those who would put out the light of the song."

Mr. Jenkins raised shadowy arms prophetically. "To kill the song is the only salvation!"

"No!" Mr. Jenkins cried to Mr. Jenkins. "You are only a mirror vision of me. You are nothing!"

Nothing   nothing   nothing

The word echoed, hollow, empty, repeating endlessly. Everywhere Meg kythed she seemed to meet a projection of an Echthros-Mr. Jenkins.

"Don't you understand that the Echthroi are your sav-

187

iors? When everything is nothing there will be no more war, no illness, no death. There will be no more poverty, no more pain, no more slums, no more starvation—"

Senex kythed through the Echthros. "No more singing!"

Proginoskes joined Senex. "No more stars, or cherubim, or the light of the moon on the sea."

And Calvin: "There will never be another meal around table. No one will ever break bread or drink wine with his companions."

Meg kythed violently against the nearest Echthros-Mr. Jenkins, "You are nothing! You're only borrowing Mr. Jenkins in order to be something. Go away! You are nothing!"

Then she was aware that the real Mr. Jenkins was trying to reach her. "Nature abhors a vacuum."

Calvin replied, "Then we must fill the vacuum. That is the only thing to do."

"How?"

"If the Echthroi are nothingness, emptiness, then that emptiness can be filled."

"Yes, but how do we fill it?"

Senex kythed calmly, "Perhaps you don't want to fill it strongly enough. Perhaps you do not yet understand what is at stake."

"I do! A little boy, my brother—what do you know about my little brother?"

Senex conveyed considerable confusion. He had a feeling for the word 'brother' because all farae are—or had been

—brothers. But 'little boy' meant nothing to him whatsoever.

"I know that my galactic host is ill, perhaps dying—"

"That's Charles Wallace! That's my little brother! He may be a galactic host to you, but to me he's just a little boy like—like Sporos." She turned her kythe from Senex and towards the wildly dancing farandolae who had surrounded another fara. This time she kythed herself towards them cautiously. How could she be sure which one was Sporos?

An Echthros-Mr. Jenkins whinnied with laughter. "It doesn't matter. Nothing matters." A harsh twang wounded the melody of the farae who were still singing.

Once again Meg felt faltering in the mitochondrion. Yadah was in pain. Suddenly she remembered the farandolae who had saved her from the Echthros when Proginoskes brought her into Yadah. Not all the farandolae had thrown in their lot with the Echthroi. Or were those who had Xed themselves that she might live the only ones who would defy the Echthroi?

She began calling urgently, "Sporos! Farandolae! Come away from the Echthroi. You will dance yourselves to death. Come to Senex and Deepen. This is what you were born to do. Come!"

Some of the farandolae faltered. Others whirled the faster, crying, "We don't need to Deepen. That's only an old superstition. It's a stupid song they sing, all this Glory, glory, glory. We are the ones who are glorious."

189

"The stars——" Meg called desperately.

"Another superstition. There are no stars. We are the greatest beings in the universe."

Ugliness seeped past Meg and to Sporos. "Why do you *want* to Deepen?"

Sporos's twingling was slightly dissonant. "Farandolae are born to Deepen."

"Fool. Once you Deepen and put down roots you won't be able to romp around as you do now."

"But——"

"You'll be stuck in one place forever with those fuddy-duddy farae, and you won't be able to run or move, ever again."

"But——"

The strength and calm of Senex cut through the ugliness. "It is only when we are fully rooted that we are really able to move."

Indecision quivered throughout Sporos.

Senex continued, "It is true, small offspring. Now that I am rooted I am no longer limited by motion. Now I may move anywhere in the universe. I sing with the stars. I dance with the galaxies. I share in the joy—and in the grief. We farae must have our part in the rhythm of the mitochondria, or we cannot be. If we cannot be, then we are not."

"You mean, you die?" Meg asked.

"Is that what you call it? Perhaps. I am not sure. But the song of Yadah is no longer full and rich. It is flaccid, its harmonies meager. By our arrogance we make Yadah suffer."

Meg felt Calvin beside Senex, urging, "Sporos, you are my partner. We are to work together."

"Why? You're no use to me."

"Sporos, we *are* partners, whether we like it or not."

Meg joined in. "Sporos! We need you to help save Charles Wallace."

"Why do we have to bother about this Charles Wallace? He's nothing but a stupid human child."

"He's *your* galaxy. That ought to make him special enough, even for you."

A cruel slashing cut between their kything, as though a great beak had cut a jagged wound. "Sporos! It is I, Mr. Jenkins. I am the teacher who is greater than all Teachers because I know the Echthroi."

Meg felt Proginoskes's kything clamp like steel.

The Echthros-Mr. Jenkins was holding Sporos, and speaking with honey-sweet words. "Do not listen to the earthlings; do not listen to the farae. They are stupid and weak. Listen to me and you will be powerful like the Echthroi. You will rule the universe."

"Sporos!" The real Mr. Jenkins's kything was not strong enough to break through the stream. "He is not Mr. Jenkins. Do not listen!"

Calvin's kythe came more strongly than Mr. Jenkins's. "There are two Mr. Jenkinses by you, Sporos, two Mr. Jenkinses kything you. You know that one is not real. Deepen, Sporos, that is where your reality lies. That is how you will find your place, and how you will find your true center."

Meg's mind's-ears were assailed by a howling which was

191

Echthroid, though it appeared to come from the pseudo-Mr. Jenkins. "Reality is meaningless. Nothing is the center. Come. Join the others in the race. Only a few more farae to surround and you will have Yadah for your own."

"Yadah will die," Meg cried. "We will all die. You will die!"

"If you come with us, you will be nothing," the Echthros-Mr. Jenkins spoke in cloying kythe, "and nothing can happen to nothing."

Sporos's long whiskers trembled painfully. "I am very young. I should not be asked to make major decisions for several centuries."

"You're old enough to listen to Senex," Meg told him. "You're old enough to listen to *me*. After all, I'm a galaxy to you. It's time for you to Deepen."

Sporos wriggled in the clasp of the Echthros-Mr. Jenkins. "Come, Sporos, fly with the Echthroi. Then you will crackle across the universe. There are too many mitochondria in creation. There are too many stars in the heavens. Come with us to naught, to nought."

"Deepen, Sporos, my child, Deepen."

"Sporos!" The Echthroid howl beat against the rhythm of Yadah. "We will make you a prince among Echthroi."

Meg felt a gust of wind, the familiar flicker of flame: Proginoskes. The cherubim flung his kything across the void of the Echthros-Mr. Jenkins, like a rope flung from cliff's edge to cliff's edge. "Sporos, all farandolae are royal. All singers of the song are princes."

192

"Nonsense. In Name only."

"The Name matters."

"Only to matter."

Proginoskes's kything was so gentle that it undercut the storm of Echthroi. "You are created matter, Sporos. You are part of the great plan, an indispensable part. You are needed, Sporos; you have your own unique share in the freedom of creation."

"Do not listen to that hideous cherubim. He's nothing but a deformed emanation of energy. We will give you no name and you will have power."

Calvin pushed in again. "Sporos, you are my partner. Whatever we do, we must do it together. If you join the wild farandolae again I am coming into the dance with you."

Sporos quivered, "To help kill the farae?"

"No. To be with you."

Meg cried, "Progo, let's go, too! We can help Calvin." In her impetuous relief at having something to do, she did not feel the cherubim pulling her back, but plunged into the irrational tarantella and was immediately swept out of control. Calvin was whirling beside Sporos, unable to pull him away from the circle closing in on the dying fara.

Meg was totally in the power of the revolving, twangling farandolae. The orbital velocity sucked her in, through the circle and against the limp trunk of the fara.

Within the deathly center of the dance it was dark; she could not image the whirling farandolae; she could not

193

kythe Calvin or Sporos. She heard only a silence which was not silence because within this vortex there was an emptiness which precluded the possibility of sound.

Caught in this anguished vacuum she was utterly powerless. She was sucked against the trunk of the fara, but the fara was now too weak to hold her up; it was she who had to hold the dying Deepened One, to give it her own life's blood. She felt it being drained from her. The fara's trunk strengthened. It was Meg who was dying.

Then arms were around her, holding her, pouring life back into her, Mr. Jenkins's arms, the real Mr. Jenkins. His strength and love filled her.

As she returned to life, the firm, rhythmic tendrils of the reviving fara caressed her. Mr. Jenkins held them both, and his power did not weaken. The murderous circle was broken. Calvin held Sporos in his arms and a tear slid down his cheek. Meg turned towards him, to comfort him.

The moment she kythed away from Mr. Jenkins and to Calvin, a new circle formed, not of farandolae, but of Mr. Jenkinses, Mr. Jenkinses swirling their deathly ring around the real Mr. Jenkins.

Meg whirled back towards him, but it was too late. Mr. Jenkins was surrounded. Meg cried, "Deepen, Sporos, it's the only hope!"

The scattered farandolae darted hither and thither in confusion. Proginoskes reached out wing after invisible wing to pull them in. There was a frightened twingle.

"Look at the Echthroi!" Proginoskes commanded. "They

are killing Mr. Jenkins as they made you kill your own
farae. Look. This is what it is like."

"Mr. Jenkins!" Meg called. "We have to save Mr. Jenkins. Oh, Sporos, Deepen, it's the second ordeal, you must
Deepen."

"For Mr. Jenkins?"

"For yourself, for all of us."

"But why did Mr. Jenkins—didn't he know what would
happen to him?"

"Of course he knew. He did it to save us."

"To save us all," Calvin added. "The Echthroi have him,
Sporos. They are going to kill him. What are you going
to do?"

Sporos turned towards Senex, the fara from whom he
had been born. He reached out small green tendrils towards
all the farandolae. "It is Deepening time," he said.

They heard a faint echo of the music which had been
such joy when Blajeny took them to witness the birth of a
star. The farae were singing, singing, strengthening. Sporos
was joining in the song. All about them farandolae were
Deepening, and adding their music to the flowing of the
song.

Meg's exhaustion and relief were so great that she forgot
Mr. Jenkins. She assumed blindly that now that Sporos and
the other farandolae were Deepening, now that the second
ordeal had been successfully accomplished, all was well;

the Echthroi were vanquished; Charles Wallace would recover; she could relax.

Then she felt Proginoskes pushing through her thoughtlessness. "Meg! You forget! There are three tests!"

She turned from rejoicing. The circle of pseudo-Mr. Jenkinses was whirling wildly about the principal, closing in on him.

Proginoskes kythed so strongly that she was pulled back into painful awareness. "We cannot let the Echthroi get Mr. Jenkins. This is the third test, to rescue Mr. Jenkins. Senex, Sporos, everybody, help us!"

Meg heard a shrill, high scream, a scream that turned into a horrible laugh of triumph. It came from Mr. Jenkins. One Mr. Jenkins. There was no longer a spiral of Echthroid Jenkinses surrounding the principal. They had closed in, and entered their prey.

Proginoskes's kything cut like a knife. "The Echthroi have him. We must get him away."

12 A Wind in the Door

The Echthros-Mr. Jenkins reached towards them. The horrible, familiar stench assailed Meg. A loathsome kything came to her in Mr. Jenkins's tones superimposed on the whine of metal rubbing against metal. "Nonsense. Of course the Echthroi haven't got me. I am Mr. Jenkins, and I took the Echthroi into me because they are right. It is not the Echthroi who are empty; it was I. They have filled me with the pleasure of the abyss of nothingness. Come let me X you, come to me, come . . ."

Sporos's long, tendrilly whiskers quivered. A faint twingling came from them, but now he was kything, his young greenery moving rhythmically, his delicate new needles and leaves and blades shimmering with the rhythm of Senex, of the singing farae, of Yadah. "Earthlings, forgive me. I will sing for you. The Echthroi cannot bear the song."

Mr. Jenkins kythed like a corkscrew. "Life as we have known it is meaningless, Margaret. Civilization has failed. Your parents know this. They are giving up."

"No, no," Calvin protested. "They're not like that, they'd never give up."

"Sing," Sporos called to the Deepening farandolae, "sing with us. Our galaxy is in danger; we must save him."

Mr. Jenkins overrode him. "There is no hope except extinguishment. Let us hasten it."

197

Meg cried through the boring of the corkscrew. "Mr. Jenkins, no! Stop it!"

Calvin joined her. "Mr. Jenkins, come back, come out of the Echthroi!"

"I am back. I am here. I am finally myself. Nothing. X-Mr. Jenkins. To be Xed is the only good."

Again Meg felt a bone-shattering wrench. Every muscle in her cried out in protest. Then she was flashed a brilliant image of Calvin tugging at Mr. Jenkins, powerful images of Calvin wrestling with a Mr. Jenkins suddenly wild and strong. Mr. Jenkins's thin, flabby arms beat at Calvin with steel-spring blows. Calvin, with his lithe wiriness, eluded most of the blows, and tried desperately to catch Mr. Jenkins by the wrists—

caught him—

The wrists became talons, became nothing. Calvin was left holding nothing. Meg heard the screeching Echthroi-laugh, and Mr. Jenkins hit Calvin a thundering blow.

Meg saw red-blackness, Calvin reeling, being pulled, sucked into the vortex of the Echthros-Mr. Jenkins.

Then the images of Calvin staggering from the blow, steadying himself, readying himself, vanished. The images were gone, but Calvin was there, was with her, was part of her. She had moved beyond knowing him in sensory images to that place which is beyond images. Now she was kything *Calvin,* not red hair, or freckles, or eager blue eyes, or the glowing smile; nor was she hearing the deep voice with the occasional treble cracking; not any of this, but—

Calvin.

She was with Calvin, kything with every atom of her being, returning to him all the fortitude and endurance and hope which he had given her.

Then she felt Proginoskes trying to get her attention and turned her kythe unwillingly towards him. "Meg, I can help Calvin, but I can't help Mr. Jenkins. You may be able to. Try to go to him. Perhaps you can still reach him."

She pulled back. If she went to the Echthroid-Mr. Jenkins, would the pain of the Echthroi take her again? There were no little farandolae to save her this time. She could not do it, could not knowingly open herself to that pain—

But Mr. Jenkins had come into the whirling circle of death for her sake. If Mr. Jenkins was possessed by Echthroi now it was because of his love for her.

She gave a sigh of acceptance of what she must do. Then she turned her kythe towards Mr. Jenkins who was somewhere in the horrible Echthroid version of himself.

"Mr. Jenkins!" She flung her kythe towards him with all her might. And now she no longer saw the thinning brown hair, the same mouse-brown as her own, or the middle-aged eyes behind the lenses of the horn-rimmed spectacles, or the sloping shoulders with the light snowfall of dandruff, but something deeper, more real, beyond, past, through the senses, something which was the true person. She was with Mr. Jenkins as she had been with Calvin, Calvin who was so important to her that she didn't dare even whisper to herself how important he was—

Mr. Jenkins, too, was real, and she was with him, kything herself entirely to him—

199

From somewhere deep inside the Echthroid version of himself he was trying to say something, he was repeating, repeating, and finally she heard, a phrase he had used earlier, "Nature abhors a vacuum." The single phrase was all he could manage.

She held on to it. If the Echthroi are nothing, and Mr. Jenkins is now part of that nothing, if Calvin is being Xed into that nothing—

"Fill it! Fill it!" came Calvin's desperate kythe. Through it came a vivid image of Charles Wallace blue and gasping, her parents standing by his bed; Dr. Louise working the emergency oxygen tank; Fortinbras lying across the threshold as though to bar death from entering the room. "Fill it!"

She was cold with desperation. "Progo! Progo, what do I do?"

She heard only an echo of Calvin's call. "Fill the vacuum. Fill it." He was fighting desperately, not for his own life but for Meg's, for Charles Wallace's, for the singing farae, for the whole of being . . .

She kythed wildly. "Progo, we passed the first test, I Named Mr. Jenkins. And the second—Sporos has Deepened. Are we failing the third test? Calvin can't hold out any longer. Do I have to go into the Echthroi? Is that what I have to do? What will you do if I fail?"

She knew. She knew what Proginoskes would do.

Calvin was weakening rapidly, unable to counter the sledgehammer blows of the Echthros-Mr. Jenkins—

She flung herself into Mr. Jenkins, trying to hold the

cruel arms, trying to pull him away from Calvin by the sheer force of her kythe.

The pain.

It came again, as she had known it would.

Agony. Red anguish pounding against her eyeballs . . .

. . . Charles Wallace was sharing in that anguish, his parents helpless as his small body convulsed in spasms of pain. They struggled to hold him, the Murrys, the Louises, to hold him during the convulsions, to give the racked frame support . . .

Fortinbras stood in the doorway growling, his hackles rising . . .

The Echthroi were—

Meg's kythe was faint, almost obliterated by pain. "Calvin—Mr. Jenkins—don't fight the Echthroi—help me fill them—"

Cold.

Cold beyond snow and ice and falling mercury.

Cold beyond the absolute zero of outer space.

Cold pulverizing her into nothingness.

Cold and pain.

She struggled.

You are not to X me, Echthroi. I fill you.

Cold.

Darkness.

Emptiness.

Nothing.

Naught.

Nought.

Echth

X

Then

Proginoskes.

A great cry. A tempest of wind. A lightning flash of fire across the cold, breaking, burning the cold and pain.

Proginoskes Xing.

Wings. All the wings. Stretched to their fullest span. Eyes. All the eyes opening and closing, opening, dimming—

Oh, no—

Going out—

No—

Flame. Smoke. Feathers flying. Proginoskes flinging his great cherubic self into the void of the Echthroi who were Xing Mr. Jenkins and Calvin and Meg—

and Charles Wallace.

Wings and flame and wind, a great howling of all the hurricanes in the world meeting and battling—

"Progo!" Her cry kythed across Yadah, and then she knew what she must do. She must do as Mr. Jenkins had done when he had broken through the mad circle of whirling farandolae and held her. She must hold the Echthroi, hold them by holding Mr. Jenkins and Calvin—by holding Charles Wallace—

Hold them, Meg. Hold them all. Put your arms around

202

them, around the Echthroi spreading their gaping, tearing nothingness across creation.

Size does not matter. You can hold them all, Charles and Calvin and Mr. Jenkins and the burning sphere of the newborn star—

She cried out, "I hold you! I love you, I Name you. I Name you, Echthroi. You are not nothing. You are."

A small white feather which was not a feather floated through the cold.

I Name you, Echthroi. I Name you Meg.
I Name you Calvin.
I Name you Mr. Jenkins.
I Name you Proginoskes.
I fill you with Naming.
Be!
Be, butterfly and behemoth,
be galaxy and grasshopper,
star and sparrow,
you matter,
you are,
be!
Be, caterpillar and comet,
be porcupine and planet,
sea sand and solar system,
sing with us,
dance with us,

rejoice with us,
for the glory of creation,
sea gulls and seraphim,
angle worms and angel host,
chrysanthemum and cherubim
(O cherubim)
Be!
Sing for the glory
of the living and the loving
the flaming of creation
sing with us
dance with us
be with us
Be!

They were not her words only.
They were the words of Senex,
of the Deepening Sporos,
of all the singing farae,
the laughter of the greening farandolae,
Yadah itself,
all the mitochondria,
all the human hosts,
the earth,
the sun,
the dance of the star whose birthing she had seen,
the galaxies,
the cherubim and seraphim,

204

wind and fire,
the words of the Glory.

Echthroi! You are Named! My arms surround you. You are no longer nothing. You are. You are filled. You are me.
You are
Meg.

"Meg!"
Her encircling arms were around Charles Wallace.
"Where—"
(Where doesn't matter.)
Here.
Here in Charles Wallace's familiar room. Meg. Calvin. Mr. Jenkins. One Mr. Jenkins. The real Mr. Jenkins.

The Murrys. Dr. Louise, her stethoscope swinging loosely about her neck, looking disheveled, exhausted, happy . . .

The twins, Dennys with a big smudge of garden earth across his face, both boys still grubby and tired from their labors.

And Charles Wallace. Charles Wallace sitting up in bed, breathing quite easily and normally. Fortinbras no longer guarded the door, which now stood invitingly open. The oxygen tank, no longer needed, was in the corner.

"Charles! Oh, Charles Wallace!" Meg hugged him, swallowing a large and unexpected sob. "Are you all right? Are you really all right?"

"He's much better," Dr. Louise said. "We know very

little about mitochondritis, but—" Her delicate little bird's voice faded off, and she looked questioningly at Meg.

So did her father. "Whatever happened—wherever you were—Charles Wallace was talking about mitochondria and farandolae in his delirium, and something which sounded like Echthroi—"

"And about you," her mother added.

Meg explained flatly, "We were in one of Charles Wallace's mitochondria."

Mr. Murry pushed his spectacles up his nose in the same gesture which his daughter used. "So he said." He looked at his youngest son. "I am not in a doubting mood."

Mrs. Murry said, "Just when we thought—when we thought it was all over—Charles Wallace gasped, 'The Echthroi are gone!' and suddenly his breathing started to improve."

"All I can say," Dennys said, "is that when Charles Wallace goes back to school, he'd better not talk the way he was doing while he was delirious."

"I don't understand any of this," Sandy said. "I don't like things I don't understand."

"If Mother and Father hadn't been so upset about Charles Wallace," Dennys glared at Meg, "they'd have been furious with you for not coming right home from school."

"Where were you, anyhow?" Sandy asked.

"Do you really expect us to swallow this stuff about your being *inside* Charles Wallace?"

"If you'd just be *realistic* for once."

"After all, we were worried, too."

206

"And then some."

They looked at Meg, then wheeled and looked at Mr. Jenkins.

Mr. Jenkins said, "Meg is quite correct. And I was with her."

The twins replied with total and stunned silence.

Finally Dennys shrugged and said, "Maybe one day someone will get around to telling us what really went on."

"I suppose since Charles is all right—"

"We'll just be glad about that. All's well that ends well and all that stuff."

"Even if everybody's holding out on us as usual."

They turned to Dr. Louise: "Charles is really okay?" "Is Charles really all right?"

Dr. Louise answered them, "It's my opinion that he'll be completely recovered in a day or so."

Meg confronted Mr. Jenkins. "Okay, but what about school? Won't the trouble there go on just as miserably as ever?"

Mr. Jenkins sounded his most acid. "I think not."

"What will you *do,* Mr. Jenkins? Can you make things different?"

"I don't know. I cannot dictate Charles Wallace's safety. He must learn, himself, to adapt. But I have less fear of the situation than I did before. After our—uh—recent experiences, the old red schoolhouse is going to be easier to enter each morning. Now I think that I am going to find upgrading an elementary school a pleasant change, and at the moment it seems a quite possible challenge."

The twins again looked astonished. Sandy asked in a deflated way, "Well, then, isn't anybody hungry?"

"We were so worried about Charles, we haven't eaten for—"

"I'd like a turkey dinner," Charles Wallace said.

Mrs. Murry looked at him, and some of the strain eased from her face. "I'm afraid I can't manage that, but I can thaw some steaks from the freezer."

"Can I come down when dinner is ready?"

Dr. Louise looked at him with her sharply probing gaze. "I don't see why not. Meg, you and Calvin stay with him until then. The rest of us will go to the kitchen to be useful. Come along, Mr. Jenkins, you can help me set the table."

When the three of them were alone, Charles Wallace said to Calvin, "You didn't say a word."

"I didn't need to." Calvin sat on the foot of Charles Wallace's bed. He looked as tired as Dr. Louise, and as happy. He put one hand lightly over Meg's. "It will be good to have a feast together, and celebrate."

Meg cried, "How can we have a feast without Progo!"

"I haven't forgotten Progo, Meg."

"But where is he?"

"Meg, he Xed himself."

"But where is he?"

(Where doesn't matter.)

Calvin's hand pressed more strongly against Meg's. "As Progo might say, he is Named. And so he's all right. The

Echthroi did not get Progo, Meg. He Xed of his own volition."

"But, Calvin——"

"Proginoskes is a cherubim, Meg. It was his own choice."

Meg's eyes were too bright. "I wish human beings
couldn't have feelings. I am having feelings. They hurt."

Charles Wallace hugged her. "I didn't imagine my dragons, did I?"

As he had intended her to, she gave a watery smile.

Immediately after dinner Dr. Louise ordered Charles
Wallace back to bed. Meg held out her arms to kiss him
good night. She knew that he was aware of her feeling of
incompleteness without Proginoskes, and, as he kissed her
cheek, he whispered, "Why don't you and Calvin go out to
the north pasture and the big rocks and look around?"

She nodded, then glanced at Calvin. Wordlessly they
slipped out to the pantry and put on ski jackets. When they
had left the house behind them, he said, "It's funny to talk
instead of kything, isn't it? I suppose we'd better get used
to it."

She walked close beside him, across the rich, newly
spaded earth of the garden. "There are things we aren't
going to be able to talk about in front of people except in
kything."

Calvin reached for one of her mittened hands. "I have a
feeling we're not supposed to talk about them too much."

Meg asked, "But Blajeny——where's Blajeny?"

Calvin's hand held hers firmly. "I don't know, Meg. I suspect that he's wherever he's been sent, Teaching."

They paused at the stone wall.

"It's a cold night, Meg. I don't think Louise will come out." He climbed the wall and moved swiftly to the two glacial rocks. The great stones loomed darkly against the sky. The grass about them was crunchy with frost. And empty.

Meg said, "Let's go to the star-watching rock."

The star-watching rock lay coldly under the brilliance of the stars. There was nothing there. A tear trickled down Meg's cheek, and she wiped it away with the back of one mitten.

Calvin put his arm around her. "I know, Meg. I want to know what's happened to Progo, too. All I know is that somehow or other, he's all right."

"I think I *know* he's all right. But my mind would like to be in on the knowing." She shivered.

"We'd better go in. I promised your parents we wouldn't stay out long."

She felt an extraordinary reluctance to leave, but she allowed Calvin to lead her away. When they reached the stone wall she stopped. "Wait a minute—"

"Louise isn't—" Calvin started, but a dark shadow slid out of the stones, uncoiled slowly and gracefully, and bowed to them.

"Oh, Louise," Meg said, "Louise—"

But Louise had dropped to the wall again and disappeared somewhere within it. Nevertheless Meg felt comforted and reassured. In silence they returned to the house. In the pantry they hung their jackets on the hooks; the door to the lab was closed. So was the door to the kitchen.

Then the kitchen door blew open with a bang.

Sandy and Dennys were at the dining table, doing homework. "Hey," Sandy said, "you don't need to be so violent."

"You could just *open* the door, you don't have to take it off its hinges."

"We didn't touch the door," Meg said. "It blew open."

Sandy slammed his Latin text shut. "That's nonsense. There's hardly any wind tonight, and what there is, is coming from the opposite direction."

Dennys looked up from his math paper. "Charles Wallace wants you to come upstairs to him, Meg. Shut the door, at any rate. It's cold."

Sandy got up and shut the door firmly. "You were gone long enough."

"Did you count the stars or something?"

"We don't have to count them," Meg said. "They just need to be known by Name."

Calvin's eyes met hers for a long moment and held her gaze, not speaking, not kything, simply being.

Then she went up to Charles Wallace.